Dear Reader,

Planning and writing this book made us think about why antiques hold a special appeal for storytellers. We find in old objects mysteries that fire the imagination. Who used that old map, which is now a wall hanging? Who cradled in their hands those coffee mugs adorned with the logo of a long-closed diner? A handmade quilt, a slide rule, old bus tokens... the objects almost tell a story by themselves. And with our beloved Blue Hill as the setting for an antiques fair, our imaginations roamed in all directions.

In *Sidetracked Suspicions,* a lot of the narrative elements converged on one important theme—more than the mystique imbued in things or the monetary value we give them, how we treat and come to care for one another is our lasting legacy. It certainly was Aunt Edie's. Her generosity in spirit continues as a model for Anne, and indeed for all of us.

Enjoy!

Jolyn and William Sharp
writing as Emily Thomas

Secrets of the Blue Hill Library

Nowhere to Be Found

Shadows of the Past

Unlocking the Truth

Theft and Thanksgiving

The Christmas Key

Off the Shelf

Gone in a Flash

All Sewn Up

If Walls Could Talk

The Rightful Owner

Cracking the Code

The Valentine Visitor

Without a Trace

Stagestruck

All That Glitters

Lights! Camera! Action!

Mum's the Word

Sidetracked Suspicions

Sidetracked Suspicions

EMILY THOMAS

Guideposts
New York

Secrets of the Blue Hill Library is a trademark of Guideposts.

Published by Guideposts Books & Inspirational Media
110 William Street
New York, NY 10038
Guideposts.org

Cover and interior design by Müllerhaus
Cover illustration by Ross Jones, represented by Deborah Wolfe, LTD
Typeset by Aptara, Inc.

Printed and bound in the United States of America
10 9 8 7 6 5 4 3 2 1

Sidetracked Suspicions

Chapter One

On a Monday morning in early June, the front door of the Blue Hill Library flew open and Wendy Pyle, in all her five-foot-one glory, stepped through, raised one hand in the air, and sang out loud for the benefit of anyone within earshot that she "had a fever that was hard to bear."

Anne Gibson was seated behind the checkout desk processing the books that had been returned over the weekend. She glanced calmly up at her friend, who held her pose, awaiting a reaction. "Good morning, Peggy Lee," Anne said and returned her gaze to her computer terminal.

Appearing somewhat deflated by Anne's mild response, Wendy shut the door behind her and stepped over to the checkout desk, heaving a canvas shopping bag onto its surface. "I suppose you want me to shush," she said.

"I've told you before that librarians don't shush," Anne replied. "That's a stereotype." A smile tugged at one side of her mouth, and she glanced over her glasses at her friend again.

Recovering her enthusiasm, Wendy leaned forward and asked, "Don't you want to know what 'fever' I'm singing about?"

"I'm guessing," said Anne, shifting a pile of books, "that, like last week and the week before, it's auction fever."

"Auction fever, baby!" Wendy cried, pumping her fist into the air. "All of Blue Hill is catching it. It's an epidemic. An epidemic of community spirit. You need to catch the fever too, Anne."

"I'm feeling sufficiently feverish, thank you. But I gather"—she gestured toward the shopping bag—"that your current bout of fever has a specific cause?"

"I was just at the bank," Wendy replied, pulling an old shoe box from the bag and removing the lid, "and Rita Sloan came out from her office to give me this." She carefully unfolded some tissue paper to reveal three small beaded purses. "They originally belonged to her grandmother before she gave them to Rita, but she says that she never uses them." Wendy ran her fingers lightly over the beads. "Aren't they gorgeous?"

Despite their obvious age, the purses appeared to be in excellent condition. Wendy carefully lifted them from the box, and the nacre and glass beads seemed to change color as Wendy moved the purses in the light.

"They're mad-money bags," Betty Bultman said from behind Wendy. Anne glanced up to see Betty looking over Wendy's shoulder with a book in her hand. "When my grandmother used to go to formal dances, her mother always made sure that she had enough cash in her mad-money bag for cab fare to get her home in case her date turned out to be a lout." She looked down at the three purses. "For the auction?" she asked, and Wendy nodded.

Taking Betty's book from her, Anne said, "That's very generous."

"Lots of people have been generous," Wendy said with a satisfied smile.

"That's what Bob says too," Betty said, referring to her husband, the mayor of their town, "but I haven't been down to the museum yet to see all the donations that have been collected." Betty retrieved the book that Anne had checked out to her.

"You should come down this afternoon," said Wendy. "The committee will be doing some sorting. It would be a good time to see everything."

Betty paused for a moment as if mentally reviewing her schedule, then smiled and said, "I believe I will." She wished Anne and Wendy a good day and left, and Wendy began to repack the purses in the tissue paper.

"Can I put these behind the desk for safekeeping?" asked Wendy, now intent on her work.

"What? Why?" Anne spoke a bit sharply. "Aren't you taking them to the museum?"

Wendy gestured to the room around them. "I've got my shift." She was one of Anne's most dedicated volunteers.

Anne frowned. "I'll be fine here alone for the few minutes that you'll need to take them down to the museum." She hesitated a moment, then said, "I don't think I want the responsibility of having them here."

Wendy shrugged. "Well, if you don't mind…"

Anne shooed Wendy toward the exit, but the library door opened before Wendy could turn the handle.

"You're back!" Anne exclaimed.

Douglas and Marian Pauthen stepped into the expansive foyer, and Wendy repeated Anne's exclamation. "You're back!" She paused, apparently trying to recall where they had gone. "California, right? To see your old Army buddies?"

Douglas nodded and Marian added, "And to see nieces and nephews."

"How was it?" Anne asked.

"Well, funny thing..." Douglas slowly shook his head. "I can't tell just quite how it happened, but you know all those young fellas I told you about? The ones I was in the service with? They've all gotten *old*!" He shook his head again as if befuddled, but he had a twinkle in his eye.

Marian poked her husband and shook her head. "We had a lovely time, Anne, thank you."

Anne and Wendy asked them a few more questions about their two-week trip then brought them up-to-date on some of the news in Blue Hill.

"Railroad Days? Auction?" Douglas asked after Wendy referred to them a couple of times. "What auction?"

"Douglas, you know they started the planning for Railroad Days before we even left," his wife said.

"I know, Mare," he responded in an apologetic tone, "but I wasn't paying that much attention. And now, even though we've only been gone for two weeks, it seems to have become the only topic in town. Although I don't believe I know many of the details. Could you enlighten me?"

Anne and Wendy looked at one another. "Wendy, you're the committee member," Anne said, offering a "you explain it" gesture. Anne knew that, while Wendy had reluctantly been pressed into service on the ad hoc planning committee for Blue Hill's Railroad Days events, she had come to really enjoy the experience.

"So you know that the basic idea is to celebrate the 150th anniversary of the arrival of the railroad in Blue Hill, right?" Wendy began with a gleam in her eye.

Douglas nodded. "Yes, I attended the talk that Mr. McCollum gave last month," he said, referring to the director of the Blue Hill Railroad Museum. "It was fascinating. I hadn't realized how important the railroad was to the early development of the town."

"Yes," said Wendy, nodding vigorously, "that was our first event. And we have others scheduled over the next few weeks. But the idea that has really exploded has been the Antique Appraisal Fair and Auction." Wendy beamed.

"Ask her whose idea that was," Anne interjected.

Wendy, never one to take the credit, waved that comment away. "It was a team effort, but the point is, in the past couple of weeks people have started to get really excited about it."

"And what all will that involve?" Douglas asked.

"This will be the culminating event of the whole Railroad Days celebration," Wendy said. "That Saturday we're going to have a daylong antique appraisal fair, so that anyone can bring in any antique they want and have it appraised for free."

"Like on that TV show," Marian said.

"Yes," Wendy continued, "like that. Do you know Miles Bridges, who runs Midtown Antiques?"

The Pauthens nodded.

"He's coordinating all the appraisers. Everyone recognizes that Mr. Bridges is the foremost authority in these parts on antiques. He'll do a lot of the appraising himself, but he has also rounded up a number of other specialty experts. Of course, he'll also be drawing on the knowledge of our local antique authorities, such as George Franklin from Franklin's Antiques, and Harriet and James Zelinski who run Minnie's Doll Hospital. And then that evening, he will cry the charity benefit auction!"

"Wendy is very proud of her new auction jargon," Anne interjected.

Wendy chuckled and shook her head. "People are donating all kinds of wonderful things for the auction. The proceeds will be divided so that half will benefit the Blue Hill Railroad Museum and half will go to the town council to distribute to other worthy causes. Oh, and before the auction, we're displaying all of the donated items at the museum. More things are going on display all the time." Once again, she pulled out the beaded purses so the Pauthens could admire them.

"How did you come to be so involved with all this, Wendy?" asked Douglas. "Are you a railroad buff?"

Wendy responded with a laugh. "I'm not, although it's been interesting to learn about." She shook her head and laughed again. "It's my children's fault. They're involved in another Railroad Days project. Hal McCollum's brainchild actually. He dreamed up the idea of collecting oral histories from older Blue Hill residents about the railroad and about the history of the town.

"He wanted to use high school students as the interviewers, so a few months ago he gave a presentation at the school, looking to recruit volunteers. Well, my daughter Hannah signed on, the other Railroad Days activities started to come together, and yours truly found herself drafted for the steering committee." Wendy smiled as she spread her hands and shrugged.

"An inspiring tale of selfless dedication," Anne said with a wink.

"Oh, shush, you," Wendy retorted. She turned back to the Pauthens. "Anyway, that's what happened while you were away, and I really hope you'll plan to come to the fair and the auction."

"Oh, we'll be there," said Douglas, "and if I know that look on my wife's face, we'll be donating something as well."

Marian glanced up at her husband and smiled. "Oh, I have some ideas," she said. "But at the moment, I still need to find something to read."

The two of them moved off to scan the shelves for new releases.

"And what about you?" Wendy asked Anne. "Have you decided what you're going to donate yet?"

Anne had been trying to think of an appropriate choice, but she still hadn't settled on anything.

When she didn't respond immediately, Wendy continued, "You know, you don't have to donate to the auction at all. You could just register to have something appraised. We've already got a hundred people signed up for the appraisal slots, and Mr. Bridges is talking about bringing in a few more experts because of the interest."

"As a matter of fact," Anne said, "I do have something I'm curious about. Aunt Edie had a collection of *matryoshka* dolls..." She paused at the quizzical look on her friend's face. "You know, those Russian nesting dolls?" Wendy nodded in recognition, and Anne continued, "Aunt Edie had some really nice ones. I'm sure they're in the attic someplace, but I haven't tried to dig them out yet. I figured I'd wait until Liddie is a little older. When I was a child, I wasn't allowed to play with them unless Aunt Edie was supervising." She smiled at the memory. "I'd pester her to show them to me often. They were a lot of fun. There was a set of Russian peasant dolls, I remember, and the smallest was a tiny little baby. Another set was of Soviet political figures. There was also a religious-themed set that Aunt Edie said was very old. Plus some others. She wrote a small book about matryoshka dolls once, did I ever tell you?"

"No, not that I recall." Wendy shook her head. "And I think I'd remember if I'd heard your aunt Edie had written a book."

"I should find my copy of that," Anne said. "Anyway, I've wondered whether those dolls might have some real value, aside from sentimental value, of course. It would be interesting to learn more about them."

Wendy nodded. "I'm sure someone at the appraisal fair can tell you all about them—what they're worth, how to take care of them." She hoisted her canvas bag over her shoulder. "All right, I'm off to the museum. I'll be back in ten minutes, if you think you can handle the crowds until then."

As she watched Wendy breeze out the door, Anne reflected that her friend was right about the level of interest that had developed around the Antique Appraisal Fair and Auction. Anne had seen a steady stream of patrons at the library there to review whatever reference materials she had about antiques. The Kovels guides were particularly popular, and at the end of the day, Anne would find them bristling with sticky notes that had been used as bookmarks. She'd made a little game out of guessing which items were being investigated. The sections covering Depression glass, silver serving sets, and antique tools seemed to be in great demand, but toys of all sorts, watches, and vinyl records were also being investigated.

The appraisal fair was a popular topic of conversation as well, and many of her patrons were eager to tell Anne about the items they intended to have appraised. Mostly, it seemed to her, people were curious about things that held more sentimental than monetary value. One woman had a set of letters her great-uncle, a professional calligrapher in the 1920s, had penned in that beautiful, flowing script. Another had a Civil War era locket with a lock of hair in it and a tiny picture of a stiffly posed young soldier. Each item came with a story, and Anne had quickly recognized the wisdom in Hal McCollum's idea of tapping this event for an outpouring of Blue Hill's living history.

* * *

Later that afternoon, Anne was behind the checkout desk when she was surprised to see Wendy, whose shift was long over, once again come through the front door of the library. "No musical entrance this time?" Anne asked with a smile.

Wendy ignored this and instead asked, "Is he here?" Anne's puzzled expression and a quick glance around the room answered Wendy's question. Shrugging, she stepped up to the desk. "Miles Bridges called me and asked if I could meet him here. I guess I got here first."

Anne's puzzled expression deepened. "Here? Why?" Surely he wasn't coming to do research, she thought. He had his own, more specialized, resources.

Wendy shook her head. "Don't know." But before she could say more, the antiques dealer came through the door wearing a broad grin and cradling a box in the crook of his arm.

"Good afternoon, ladies," he said, a twinkle in his eye. "I have something here that I think will be of interest to you."

The two women exchanged a glance as he set the box on the checkout desk with great care.

He seemed to be trying to control his own excitement before continuing. "I should explain that I have been approached by a certain individual who wishes to make a donation to the auction." He gestured toward the box. "But this generous person had two requests to make. Before I share those requests, however, let's just have a look." He removed the lid of the box and gently parted several layers of bubble wrap and tissue.

Anne and Wendy crowded in close behind Miles and looked over his shoulder. Nestled in the box was a vase that appeared to be of Asian design. It looked very old and was a little over a foot tall, with a scene of flowers and birds showing in the narrow section exposed.

Anne glanced from the vase to Miles, who gazed down at it with an expression akin to a new grandfather.

"I'm going to leave it in the box," he said, even speaking in a hushed tone. "I don't want to handle it unnecessarily."

"It's lovely," Anne offered, feeling that some praise was called for, but after Mr. Bridges remained silent for a few moments, she finally prodded, "Who is the donor?"

"Ah well," said Miles, recovering himself, "that's the first of the requests. The donor wishes to remain anonymous."

He looked at Wendy as he said this, and she shrugged. "I guess that's okay. We hadn't really made provision for something like that, but I don't see a problem. *You* know who the donor is and can, you know, vouch for it." Wendy gestured toward the vase.

Miles nodded again but said, "I'm not an expert in Chinese porcelain, but yes, I'm arranging to have it examined by someone who's a specialist in this area."

There was another moment of silence, and Anne asked, "You said the donor has two requests. What's the other?"

"The donor has asked," said Miles, "to designate a specific beneficiary for the proceeds of this particular piece." He looked at Anne. "In fact, the donor wants it auctioned to benefit the Blue Hill Library."

When neither Anne nor Wendy responded immediately, Miles continued, "The thing is, this vase is likely to be the most valuable piece we have in the auction—by far. As I say, this isn't my area of expertise. But I've seen enough to be fairly confident that the donor is correct to estimate the vase's value at ten thousand dollars."

Chapter Two

Anne took a step back and tucked her hands under her arms. She looked at Miles. "Seriously?"

"I'm quite serious. Look at the quality," he said. "And it's my belief that the piece is several hundred years old. But I'm going to arrange to have it examined by someone who's an expert."

Anne turned to Wendy. "But that's not how the auction works, right? Donors can't dictate where the money goes. The income that doesn't go to the museum is supposed to be awarded by the town council."

Wendy exhaled a long breath. "You're right," she said, "that's how it's organized." She looked at Miles. "And if we allowed every donor to name their own beneficiary…well, I don't know how we'd keep track of it all."

"Plus, you wouldn't have a fair distribution of the income," Anne said.

Miles rested his hand lightly on the box. "But the donor is very insistent that it benefit the library specifically."

"Then why doesn't he just sell the vase and give the money to the library?" Wendy asked.

Miles hesitated. "I can't really speak to his thinking, but I have the impression that the public nature of the donation is somehow important."

Wendy gazed thoughtfully at the vase for a few moments and then looked back at Miles. "What do you think?"

"I think you should accept the donation," he said promptly. "The request doesn't violate the spirit of the auction, which is to benefit local organizations. And having a valuable piece in the mix can raise the excitement level of the whole event. You can even end up with higher bids across the board, when the crowd is really worked up."

"But it's not fair to the other donors," Anne protested. "You're changing the rules for this one person."

Miles shrugged. "The committee could set a threshold. Anyone who donates something valued above, say, five thousand dollars may also designate their beneficiary, if they wish. There wouldn't be that many to keep track of, and you might even encourage some other valuable donations. So far, we don't have anything else that meets that threshold."

"I'm going to have to take it up with the committee," Wendy said. "But, well, a donation like this would clearly be a boon to the library. I don't think anyone is going to want to stand in the way of something like that, even if it does mean bending the rules a bit."

Anne listened in a bit of a daze while Miles explained that he'd already had an assistant take a series of photographs of the vase that he'd be e-mailing to an expert. She hoped that Wendy was paying more attention than she was. But it was clear, even in her stupefied state, that Miles was eager to put the vase on display along with the other items that had been donated for the auction.

"Please let me know as soon as the committee has made its decision," he said to Wendy. "For now, I'm going to keep it in the museum's secure storage area."

"Actually," said Wendy, looking at her watch, "the committee members are gathering at the museum in about half an hour. We're supposed to be sorting through the donations, but perhaps we can discuss the question then."

Miles smiled happily and then turned to Anne. "I want to assure you that the vase will be well protected at the museum. Hal has hired extra security for the period leading up to the auction. You can be comfortable leaving it there."

He seemed to want some sort of reassurance from Anne, so she offered a vague assent. Then Miles told Wendy he'd see her at the museum, closed up the box again, and carried it away as tenderly as he had brought it in.

Once he was gone, Wendy turned to Anne and said with a broad smile, "Well, talk about auction fever! What a wonderful thing for the library!" Anne didn't reply immediately, and Wendy gave her a puzzled look. "What's up with you? The way you were raising all those objections, you'd almost think you didn't want the donation."

Anne looked down at the checkout desk and began to drum her fingers lightly on the surface.

"Well, what is it?" Wendy demanded. "What's the problem?"

Anne sighed and glanced around to see who else was in the library. There were no patrons in their vicinity, but she still kept her voice low. "I don't know. It's just... that's an awfully generous gift. I'd feel better knowing who it was coming from."

"That's *all*?" Wendy's tone betrayed her skepticism.

"No. I mean, look, I realize it's premature to say this, but... in my experience, large gifts can often come with large expectations. The donor is anonymous now, but that doesn't mean that he or she is going to stay in the shadows once this vase has been auctioned. I don't want to feel pressured to run the library a certain way just because someone made a big donation."

Wendy looked thoughtful. "Okay, I can see where that might be a concern. But if this mystery donor really did want to have a say in things, wouldn't they have to make that clear up front? I mean, it would have to be a condition of accepting the donation, if they really wanted to make it stick. Right now it appears that the donor is making this gift with no strings attached. He or she can't very well turn around and claim otherwise after the fact. They would have no grounds to do so."

"Technically, yes," Anne conceded, "but that wouldn't stop them from badgering me to run things in a particular way, or from bad-mouthing the library if I don't. Making a big donation gives people a sense of entitlement, whether it's justified or not. And you heard what Mr. Bridges said—the donor wants their gift to be 'public.' I take that to suggest they might be planning to use public opinion as leverage."

Wendy frowned and looked ready to pursue the argument but then looked at her watch and seemed to change her mind. "I think you're looking too far into the mouth of this gift horse. The library is a good thing. People want to support it. Have a little faith. But in any event, I've gotta get down to the museum to meet the other committee members."

* * *

All the next day, Anne pondered the mysterious donation, trying to understand the source of her unease and mulling over the words of her friend. It was true—the library was a good thing and people did want to support it. She'd learned that already. Blue Hill had been without a library for a very long time, and that seemed to make the residents all the more grateful to have one now.

And they had it now thanks to the generosity of Anne's great-aunt Edie, a beloved figure in Anne's life. Following Aunt Edie's death, as stipulated in her will, part of her enormous Victorian home was to be converted into a library, which the town sorely needed. She had named Anne to be the librarian. At the time, Anne was a widowed mother of two in Brooklyn who had just been laid off from her job at the New York City Public Library, so she swallowed whatever reservations she'd had about returning to her childhood home and had moved back to Blue Hill to take on the challenge of starting and operating a small-town library.

The community, she'd found, embraced their new library. She was proud of the collection she had built and the programming she was developing—and the way in which the library was becoming a true center of civic life.

Was that part of the problem, she wondered? Was she so proud of what she'd accomplished on her own that she felt threatened by such a sizable donation from an unknown source? In many ways, the library felt like something she and Aunt Edie had built together—for Anne felt that Aunt Edie's spirit and legacy inspired all that happened there. So was Anne now afraid that some outsider was going to come and steal some of Aunt Edie's glory?

The thought bothered her, and she fussed with the objects on her desk as she pondered the possibility. Before she could obsess over it too long, though, the library door banged open and her children, nine-year-old Ben and five-year-old Liddie, charged in.

Already on edge, Anne jumped up at the commotion and instinctively began to raise a finger to her lips, but before she did, she recalled her exchange with Wendy the previous morning about shushing librarians. Instead she offered her kids a quick wave and a smile. Liddie ran into her mother's arms with a shriek of glee.

School had only been out for summer break for a few days, and Alex Ochs had graciously offered to let Anne share a teenage babysitter at his house for a few hours each day over the next couple of weeks. Anne still hadn't decided whether or not she wanted to hire a sitter full time over the summer to stay with the kids upstairs in their private living quarters while she worked downstairs in the library, or if they could get by with her checking on them frequently.

Close behind Ben, Ryan Slater stepped through the door with a soccer ball under one arm and a backpack laden with books over his shoulder. He set the ball down and started pulling library books out of the pack for return.

Ryan lived with his uncle, Alex Ochs, one of Anne's high school friends, and lately he had been spending many afternoons and evenings with the Gibsons while Alex, like Wendy, volunteered with the Railroad Days committee.

Anne was pleased that Ben and Ryan had hit it off. In high school, she and Alex had been a steady couple, but they lost touch when she left Blue Hill for college. Since her return, she'd been happy to find that Alex was still a good friend. In fact, he was the contractor who had handled the renovations that turned Aunt Edie's home into a library. Ben's friendship with Ryan in those early days had also eased Anne's fears about her children's adjustment to a new environment, one that was very different from the Brooklyn neighborhood they had known.

"Mom, can we go out and play in the park? For just a little bit?" Ben asked.

"Me too, Mommy?" Liddie pleaded.

"You want to go to the park too?" Anne asked, knowing that Liddie wanted to play with her brother—and that Ben and Ryan probably wanted to play by themselves. "But I have some books that need reading here. Do you think you could help me with that?"

Still young enough to be tractable, Liddie nodded happily, and Anne smiled at Ben and Ryan, telling them to run along.

Anne settled Liddie in a chair with a stack of books, but she had barely returned to her own work when Hal McCollum, the director of the railroad museum, walked in. She greeted him warmly but with a puzzled expression on her face. "Are you looking for Wendy? I thought she was with you at the museum."

Hal nodded. "Oh yes, I just left her there. The committee is still trying to sort through all the donations. We thought we could do it in one session yesterday, but it turned out to be too much. I'm not entirely certain that we'll even finish today." He paused, and then said, "But I've left them to it for a moment to come to see you, Anne."

Hal was a regular visitor to the library's History Room, but his behavior today seemed a bit odd. Anne smiled and cocked an eyebrow.

He seemed at a loss for how to continue for a moment, and then said, "I suppose Wendy told you that the committee has decided to bend the rules on the auction and accept the vase?"

Anne nodded. Wendy had told her on the phone the night before. After a moment, she said, "Thank you." She was still feeling conflicted about the donation, but she realized that the committee members had acted to support the library.

"Well, so Miles Bridges was eager to put it on display right away. He's very excited about this piece, as I guess you know. We rearranged some cabinets, and you'll be pleased to hear that it's now displayed quite prominently."

Anne smiled but couldn't bring herself to thank him again, since she was not at all sure she was pleased to hear this.

Hal seemed so caught up in some unease of his own that he didn't notice hers. "The thing is, I've been thinking about that vase all day. It's such a valuable item, and quite a responsibility." He produced a folded sheet of paper from the inside pocket of his sport coat. "So I was wondering if you'd be willing to sign this consent form. Just in case, you know, something happens. Because I just can't in good conscience let the museum assume that sort of risk."

The request took Anne by surprise. In fact, she felt rather dismayed, and she stood frowning down at the form for so long that Hal began to show signs of anxiety. But he stood his ground until she finally said, "But how can I consent? The vase itself doesn't belong to the library. We're just supposed to get the proceeds from its sale at auction."

Hal McCollum was nodding vigorously before she even finished speaking. "Yes, I talked that all over with Miles, and he's arranging to have the anonymous donor sign a consent form as well. But he and I agree that it would be best if you *both* sign a form, just to be safe." Evidently he could now sense her distress, because after a moment he added in a quieter tone, "I can see you're uncomfortable, Anne, so I'm sorry to ask, but I have a responsibility to the trustees of the museum. And after all, it's just a precaution."

Anne sighed. "I know, Hal. It's your job to think about these things." She spread the paper on the desk and reached for a pen. "As I say, I don't see that I have any standing to give consent, but I don't wish to be an obstructionist either." She signed her name to the form.

Hal thanked her profusely, and Anne could tell it was a relief to him to have the business settled. "Well," he said with a much jauntier air, "I should get back and help my fellow committee members with the sorting. It's going to be an amazing event, Anne, and this vase will be one of the highlights. I hope you'll come by soon and see how it's displayed. "

As he left, Anne wished she could share his enthusiasm.

Chapter Three

"Have you seen the paper?"

For once, Anne was not behind the checkout desk when Wendy arrived at the library the next morning. Anne had left Sherri Deveraeux, one of her volunteers, to handle the desk while Anne shelved some new books in the Children's Room. Wendy had bounded up the stairs to find her and was now waving a copy of the *Blue Hill Gazette*, the town's weekly newspaper, which had come out that day.

Anne, on her knees at a low shelf, looked up at her friend with a smile. "No, I haven't had time yet. Why?"

Wendy flourished the paper's front page before Anne's eyes. "Ta-da!"

Anne had to scan it for a moment before she registered the headline and story in the lower left: "Valuable Vase Donated to Library."

"Oh no."

Wendy lowered the paper with a look of dismay. "What, you didn't know about this?" When Anne shook her head, Wendy continued, "I wondered why there was no quote from you, but how could Grace run a story like this without telling you?"

With a sigh, Anne closed her eyes and hung her head. "It's my fault. She left me a voice mail message yesterday, but I haven't called her back yet." She placed her hands on her thighs and finally stood. "Though, in my own defense, she didn't actually say she was calling about a story. I thought it was just a social call." She reached out and took the paper from Wendy. "She probably just heard about it yesterday, and Tuesday is her deadline." She began to scan the story.

"Even still," Wendy said in a slightly aggrieved tone, "she must have gotten the story from Miles or Hal. They're both quoted."

"Oh, word's already getting around." Anne flipped to an inside page where the story was continued. "I already had people in here at the end of the day yesterday asking me about it."

Wendy gazed at her friend with concern. "You're still worried about this donation?" When Anne didn't respond immediately, Wendy continued, "You could still refuse it, you know, even if it *has* been in the paper. There's no law that says you have to accept it."

Anne closed the paper, looked at her friend, and sighed. "I can't do that. I'm still concerned, but I don't see how I can refuse it. Hal McCollum was talking to me yesterday about his responsibility to the museum. Well, I have a responsibility to the library, and I can't in good conscience refuse such a significant donation, at least not without better reasons than my own vague misgivings." She screwed up her mouth in dismay. "But it doesn't mean I don't still have them."

"Maybe you should talk with Reverend Tom?"

Anne nodded. "Yeah, I thought I'd go see him tomorrow, as a matter of fact." She looked up and smiled. "But what about you? Did the committee finally finish all that sorting last night?" As she spoke, she began leading Wendy back downstairs to the first floor of the library.

Wendy's tone was rueful. "No, still not done. It's taking an awful lot longer than we expected. And more stuff keeps coming in. But we can't keep meeting every night. We have our own lives, after all."

"So when do you gather again?" Anne asked, thinking about Alex. They'd reached the bottom of the stairs, where Anne picked up a copy of *Publishers Weekly* to read the prepress reviews when she had a chance.

"The next day that we can all meet is Saturday, and then not until the evening," Wendy said with a sigh. "This has been a great experience, but I'll be glad when it's done."

"You've certainly earned your vacation."

Wendy looked at Anne blankly. "My gosh, there's been so much to do, I completely forgot about our vacation."

Anne raised an eyebrow. "You're still going to Maine, aren't you?"

"Oh yes. We got a great rate on a cabin near Acadia National Park. It's perfect for a family of our size. The only thing is, I'll miss a week of preparations in the run-up to the appraisal fair and auction. I've warned the committee this will be happening but still..."

Anne slapped at the air. "You're so organized, the event will practically run itself." Wendy shook her head, but Anne went on, "I mean it. All the work you put into the Web site and publicizing—no, *creating* antiques fever—I doubt half the things would have come in for donation or for the appraisal fair if not for you."

Wendy smiled awkwardly. After a moment, she said, "Speaking of stuff still coming in, what about you? Will you be donating something? What about those dolls that you mentioned?"

"Oh yes, I have to look for the matryoshka dolls. But I'm not donating those to the auction, I'm just having them appraised. They have too much sentimental value for me to part with them." Anne grew thoughtful. "But you're right, I still have to decide what to donate. You know, I think I have more than one copy of Aunt Edie's book about the matroyshka dolls. Maybe I could donate a copy of that?"

"I think something written by Edie would be a great choice," said Wendy. "It would almost make her a part of the Railroad Days."

* * *

Anne had actually done more than plan to visit Reverend Tom on Thursday, she'd called him and made an appointment. Which felt strange to her, since she saw and spoke with him on a regular basis, but in this case it seemed the thing to do.

Anne had attended the Blue Hill Community Church growing up, but the pastor from those days had long since retired. When she returned to Blue Hill, she found that Reverend Tom Sloan had been serving the congregation for a decade and was well loved by all its members. She quickly learned why, as he was both wise and compassionate. He'd proven to be both a good friend and good counselor to Anne.

If he found it odd that Anne scheduled this visit, he gave no sign of it as he greeted her warmly and ushered her into his office. He sat down opposite her and gazed at her with an inquiring expression. Anne realized that she had no idea how to start. After several moments in which her mouth worked but she failed to figure out what to say, the absurdity of the situation struck both of them, and they burst out laughing.

"Well," Reverend Tom said with a kindly smile, "at least it's not so bad you can't laugh about it." After a pause, he continued, "Does it perhaps have something to do with this vase I hear so much about?"

With the topic broached, Anne was able to pour out all her concerns and hesitations both about this generous gift and about her suspicions concerning her own motivations in resisting it. "And I've prayed and prayed, Reverend Tom," she concluded, "but I still don't have an answer."

"Well," he replied, "prayer is a good thing, of course, but it doesn't absolve you of the responsibility for making your own decisions."

Anne nodded in rueful recognition.

"Accepting such a large gift does come with responsibility," he continued, "and I think that you are justified, even correct, in wishing to... take care in such a decision." The pastor shifted in his chair. "And of course, I can't make your decision for you either. But two things come to mind that I'll share. The first is that I've been in your position, and I can understand your concern. We've had some folks who have made large donations and seemed to think they'd somehow bought stock in the church as a result. There have been a couple of times when things got unpleasant, but the fact remains that the church's mission is larger than the personal concerns of individuals. The church manages to continue just fine despite these disagreements."

He paused and Anne nodded.

"The second thing," he continued, "is more of a confession, because I have struggled in the past with the same concerns as you. I, too, find myself suspicious when someone wishes to make a large donation to the church. I have had to learn over the years to set that aside and cultivate an attitude of faith. Donors give because they believe in the work of the church, even those who sometimes want to have a say in how that work gets done."

Anne nodded again. "Wendy made a similar point. I guess I'm being a bit of a doubting Thomas, aren't I?" Reverend Tom remained silent while Anne worked through her thoughts. She could feel the knot of anxiety in her stomach starting to loosen. "Well, I guess I'd better stop trying to stick my hand in the wounds."

And she did feel better as she drove back to the library. She couldn't help speculating on the identity of the mystery donor. For some reason she envisioned a formidable dowager, her hair tinted blue and set to sweep dramatically to the right, and wearing large pearl earrings and necklace and a sable coat. Someone who had fallen in love with the Beat poets in the fifties and had loved poetry ever since. Drawing this mental image helped Anne to see the donor as more of a kindly benefactor than the controlling puppet master she'd feared.

If her concerns were not gone completely, at least they had settled down a bit, and she hoped they would eventually disappear altogether.

It was with a lighter heart that she re-entered the library.

"Oh, Mrs. Gibson," said Remi Miller, one of Anne's two part-time employees. "You just missed him."

Anne looked back over her shoulder. She hadn't noticed anyone leaving as she entered. "Missed who?"

Remi shrugged. "He didn't leave his name. But guess what? He wanted to talk to you about buying your vase outright. He said he thought he could guarantee a price that would be bigger than what you'd get at auction. Isn't that exciting? I assume he'll be back."

Anne pursed her lips and said nothing.

* * *

Despite the news of the mystery buyer, who did not return over the next couple of days, Anne found herself coming to terms with the idea of the donation. By Saturday, she decided that she really ought to have a better idea of just what this vase was. She hadn't had a good look when Miles Bridges brought it by the library, so she decided to take Ben and Liddie down to the railroad museum to see the vase and all the other items that had been donated for the auction.

Since Ben was interested in trains—he had a small collection of model train cars—they had visited the museum on a number of previous occasions. As Anne and the kids stepped through the entrance this time, though, they were astounded at its transformation.

Normally a fairly quiet space, today the museum was packed with visitors, and the lively chatter filled the air with excitement and anticipation. The usual entry fee had been waived so people could see the items to be auctioned, and there were signs everywhere explaining both the auction and the Railroad Days celebration. Many of the exhibits had been removed in order to make room to display the items donated for the auction. These were crowded into cases with only a minimum of signage, but Anne noticed many of her neighbors pointing out the objects they had donated and eagerly explaining their significance.

The display was a bit haphazard—the result, Anne suspected, of the unanticipated high level of interest—but it was vibrant, varied, and intriguing. More signs encouraged visitors to take notes on objects that they might like to bid on when the auction was held, and the museum had set out scrap paper for that purpose.

Anne scanned the packed display cases, looking without success for the vase. Just as she was beginning to wonder if it was there at all, she spotted it in its own separate case, set apart from the others. The plexiglass case sat atop a four-foot-high base and had its own interior light, and the vase was displayed to dramatic effect. The museum had posted a laminated copy of the story from the *Blue Hill Gazette* on a stand nearby.

A number of people stood admiring the vase, but they quietly moved away when Anne approached, leaving her feeling exposed. Anne fought down her desire to run away and, clutching the hands of her children, stepped up to examine the vase.

She was surprised that it didn't look that special. It was beautiful, certainly, colorful and vibrant with images that looked Chinese. But she wouldn't have picked it out as a ten-thousand-dollar vase. She felt slightly disappointed and chastised herself. After all her fretting about the value of the donation and the identity of the mystery donor, she now worried that the value might have been overstated?

Someone behind her called, "Anne!" She turned to see Hal McCollum approaching from across the room with a broad smile on his face. "I'm so glad you've come down to have a look. What do you think?"

"It's…it's very striking," she fumbled. Liddie began tugging on her hand, and Anne released her.

Liddie simply stepped up to the vase display to get a closer look, but Ben gestured toward the far end of the hall. "Can I go look at the layouts?" he asked. The museum had two very elaborate model train layouts that were Ben's favorite exhibit.

"I'm not sure they're there, sweetie," she said, and looked at Hal.

"Actually, they are." He smiled down at Ben, and looking up again at Anne, he added, "They were just too large to move. Ben, we've had some donations of Lionel and American Flyer model train cars, just behind the layouts in the display case there, if you want to have a look."

Anne nodded to Ben, who scampered off. Liddie, meanwhile, was circling round and round the vase, studying it intently.

"I hadn't realized it would be quite so...prominent," Anne said, worried that it might sound like a criticism.

Hal seemed to take it as a compliment. "Oh yes, it's quite the star of the show," he said with satisfaction. "As soon as Miles Bridges showed it to me, I thought this display case would be perfect for it. I can't tell you how many people we've had scrutinizing it just as carefully as your little girl here." He smiled down at Liddie, who ignored him.

Instead, she looked up at her mother with a gleam in her eye. "Look, Mommy," she said with excitement, "it tells a story." She led Anne and Hal both on a tour round the vase, narrating a complicated tale of a man on a donkey and a bird as big as a horse that she saw in the images.

When she was done, Hal chuckled. "Actually, that's not far from the interpretation that Miles gave of the images, though his terminology was different. You see, these figures depicted in the vase are the Eight Immortals of ancient Chinese mythology."

Liddie looked proud that she had successfully read the vase.

Hal McCollum smiled. "And apparently it's quite rare to find them all together like this. The crane you see here—this big bird, Liddie—symbolizes long life, and this larger figure on the bird is, according to Miles, Shou Lao, the god of longevity."

Anne leaned in and looked more closely at the vase.

Hal pointed with his pencil at the lower portion of the vase. "Look at the delicate brush work here in the willow tree and the clouds and the harmonious color of the clothing. This vase is from the Qing dynasty, a period from the seventeenth century to the early twentieth century, when artisans produced porcelains and textiles of exceptional quality."

Anne looked up at Hal, her eyebrows raised in surprise, and he blushed.

"Or at least, that's what Miles said," he admitted. "I really have no idea."

Anne made herself smile back. "Me either."

"But we'll take good care of it, Anne. You have nothing to worry about."

* * *

For the rest of the weekend, the vase was a constant topic of conversation for Liddie. She was used to seeing images and stories in a book, but to find one on an object like a vase was a revelation to her. She made up her own stories to continue the tale she had read on the vase.

Anne felt more and more at peace with the idea of the donation. She suspected that Liddie's delight in the vase was affecting her, but she decided it was for the better. She would let a little child lead her.

One of the places that Liddie wanted to lead her was back to the museum to see the vase again. Anne explained to Liddie that the vase wasn't really theirs and that in a few weeks somebody would buy it and take it away. Liddie accepted that, but she also understood that, in the meantime, the vase was still on display in the museum, and she was eager to go back and see it again.

On Monday afternoon, Anne relented. Ben and Ryan were playing soccer, so Anne declared that she and Liddie would have a "girls' trip" to the museum.

It was a warm day but not too hot, and on their stroll, Anne told Liddie the names of all the flowers they passed. They had stopped to look at a particularly beautiful garden, when Alex Ochs surprised them by popping up behind a picket fence.

"I thought I heard familiar voices," he said, smiling.

"What in the world are you doing down there?" Anne asked, craning her neck to look over the fence.

Alex pointed to a rotted post. "I've had quite a busy day, thanks to you."

"Me?"

Alex nodded. "Well, to be more specific, that vase."

"Oh?" In an instant, Anne's guard came back up, but before she could protest that it wasn't *her* vase, Alex explained.

"I was doing some work at the museum—can you believe they need *more* display cabinets already?—when a gentleman started grilling me about building a special case for shipping something fragile. He was holding his hands like this." Alex mimed holding what looked to Anne like a basketball. "He didn't mention the vase, but he didn't have to. All of his specs and conditions took us ten minutes to lay out. Threw me off my schedule." Alex consulted his watch. "Speaking of which, I gotta run if I'm going to watch the boys at soccer practice."

"Thanks so much, Alex," Anne said, looking down at Liddie and gently guiding her back toward the sidewalk. "With the boys at soccer, we're able to have a little girl time today."

They waved and continued their walk.

Anne was pleased to find the museum much less crowded than it had been on Saturday. As soon as they arrived, Liddie dashed over to the vase, but Anne merely glanced at it before moving toward the other items that had been donated, especially the old model trains, which Ben wanted to bid on at the auction. She hadn't had a chance to examine the rest of the items on Saturday, and she was curious what she would find.

She roamed along the display cases looking for the names of people she knew, while part of her mind wondered if she could get Miles Bridges to give her copies of the photographs he'd taken of the vase. If Liddie couldn't have the vase itself, perhaps she would like to have some pictures of it.

As Anne looked and pondered, Hal McCollum once again emerged from the back room to greet her.

"Back again?"

She smiled. "I didn't have a chance to look at all this the other day." She gestured toward the case before her. "It's amazing what people have donated. I see that some of these things are even related to the railroad."

Hal's face lit up at his favorite topic. "Yes, quite a few, actually. To tell you the truth, there are one or two cases where I'd prefer to have the article itself donated to the museum, rather than the money from auctioning it off." He dropped his voice to a conspiratorial tone. "In fact, I've suggested as much to one or two donors, and I'm pleased to say that they have agreed. You don't think that's wrong, do you?"

Anne thought of her own doubts about the vase. "Of course not. They made the donation to benefit the museum. You've just provided some guidance on how they can best do that."

Hal gave her a somewhat relieved smile, and Liddie came rushing up. "Mommy, Mommy!" she cried, flushed with excitement. "The vase is telling a different story! There's a different man now!"

Anne and Hal exchanged a puzzled glance, but they followed Liddie over to the vase. Anne tried to see if she could tell what Liddie was talking about, but she had never given the vase the kind of scrutiny her daughter had.

When she glanced at Hal again, however, she saw that he was staring intently into the case and his face had blanched. Anne looked again at the vase. It was the same size, as far as she could tell, and around the vase were the Chinese figures... but there was no longer a crane floating among the clouds, and more telling, the man on the donkey was gone.

"Oh my," Hal said in a faint voice, swallowing with apparent difficulty. "I think we'd better call Miles."

Chapter Four

Officer Michael Banks looked from Anne to Hal McCollum to Miles Bridges. "So you're saying that someone has taken the vase that was in here and replaced it with this one?"

Miles nodded. "That appears to be the case."

Miles had arrived at the museum within half an hour of Hal's call, and he'd brought with him the photographs he'd taken of the vase. As soon as he saw the one in the display case, his face fell, but they nevertheless carefully compared the vase to the pictures. Even Anne could tell that it was not the same vase.

The next step had been to call the police.

Anne was relieved that Michael Banks was one of the responding officers. He and his wife were good friends of Anne's in high school, and she'd renewed her friendship with them since returning to Blue Hill.

But now Michael seemed to be carefully modulating his voice to keep out any hint of incredulity. "Why would someone do that?"

"You will probably find," Miles replied, "when you examine this vase, that it is worth considerably less than the one that has been stolen."

"But why a replacement?" Michael persisted. "Why not just steal the valuable one?"

Miles shrugged. "I can only assume it was to delay the discovery of the crime."

Michael looked down at his notebook. "And yet it doesn't seem to have done so, does it?" He looked back up at Anne. "You saw the missing vase here in this case on Saturday, yes?" Anne nodded, and Michael looked at Hal McCollum. "And that's the last time anyone can say for sure that it was there?" Hal nodded in his turn. "But even still, that means it must have gone missing sometime in the last forty-eight hours. So it doesn't appear that the... decoy hid the crime for very long."

"A lucky break for us, then," said Miles.

Michael nodded, but Anne felt he was reserving judgment. "Now, Mr. Bridges, you say that this vase here is worth less than the one that was stolen?"

"Oh no, I don't know that. I'm just assuming. I'll have to have it examined by an expert to be certain. But I'll start by taking it back to my shop to take photographs and examine it under better conditions."

Michael was already shaking his head before Miles finished speaking. "I'm sorry, Mr. Bridges. This vase is evidence now. I can't allow you to take it anyplace."

Miles was nonplussed. "I... I see. Well, then I'm afraid I can't be of much help on the question of its worth. Not without examining it and consulting my expert."

Michael looked at him thoughtfully. "And this missing vase had already been examined by your expert?"

"Well, she just took a preliminary look." Miles again seemed at a loss. "She's based in Philadelphia but consults with me regularly and lately has been coming in about one day a week. She hasn't seen the vase in person yet, but she has the pictures. I e-mailed them to her so she could start her research." He fanned out the photographs that he'd brought and which he'd been clutching all this time. "That's how she had made a preliminary determination of the vase's value."

Michael looked keenly down at the photos. "May I take these? They might be great help in the investigation."

Miles hesitated for just a fraction of a second before saying, "Of course, yes, of course. Whatever I can do to help."

"And you say your expert can make an evaluation based on pictures like these?" Michael continued as he handed them off to an officer who was assisting him. "I could arrange for our photo lab to take some pictures of the new vase."

"Well, I...I don't want to make any promises on her behalf, but I'll be happy to ask her. She might well be able to tell you something."

"We'd appreciate that," Michael said blandly. "Now then, what can you tell us about the person who donated the vase? I recall the newspaper said it was an anonymous donation, but of course we'll need to know this person's name."

Miles drew himself up. "I'm sorry, Officer, I cannot tell you that without checking with the donor first. It's a matter of honoring the confidence of a client."

They all looked at him in surprise. "Mr. Bridges," said Michael, "this is a police investigation. Anonymity is not an option."

Miles deflated again. "I...I realize that. But may I at least ask first? I'm sure that under the circumstances, my client will agree.

And if not, well, I promise to tell you anyway. But I would just feel better if I could check first. I'll attempt to reach them right away."

Michael looked at him thoughtfully for a long moment before he said, "Okay. But I will hold you to your promise to tell us, whether your client gives you permission or not."

Miles nodded.

"In that case, I'll expect to hear from you within twenty-four hours with the donor's name."

* * *

Anne called Alex and asked him to watch Ben after the soccer game. After Michael Banks's initial questions, she'd been given a statement form and asked to write down as many details as she could remember about her visits on both Saturday and today, while they were still fresh in her mind. Unfortunately, keeping Liddie amused while she did so had not helped her concentration.

Meanwhile, the police had conducted their own investigation. Two of them took pictures of the display case and the decoy vase and then dusted them for fingerprints. Finally, the vase was carefully put into a plastic evidence bag and then into a box for protection.

Other officers quizzed Hal McCollum about museum staff and procedures—who had access and when, what the security arrangements were like, and so on. Anne heard Michael tell Hal that all of his employees and volunteers would need to be interviewed, and then almost as an afterthought, Michael turned to Miles Bridges and told him that his employees would need to be interviewed as well, given his shop's involvement in the donation of the vase. After a pause, Miles nodded.

When Michael seemed finished with Hal and Miles, Anne walked up to him and asked, "Do you know how much longer this is going to take? I need to get Liddie home and feed her dinner." She nodded toward her daughter.

Michael looked concerned. "Oh goodness, I'm sorry, Anne. Yes, I think it's fine for you to go now. I may have some more questions for you at some point, but I can come by the library. And of course, we'll keep you informed about the status of the investigation."

Anne cocked her head in question.

"As the victim," Michael explained.

"Victim!" Anne exclaimed. "It's not my vase. It's still the property of the donor until someone buys it at the auction. "Or, I don't know, maybe it belongs to the town or something in the interim. But not me."

"But you signed a consent form to have it on display here," Michael said, holding up the document in question.

Her eyes widened. "Yes, but so did the donor," she said quickly. "Or, at least, that's what Hal said was going to happen. I just signed it to make Hal feel better." Now she wished she hadn't.

"Well, yes, the donor signed one as well." Michael flashed another piece of paper before putting it away again.

"Wait," Anne said, "if you have the donor's signature, then you know who the donor is." She glanced at Miles Bridges, who was off to one side, talking on his cell phone.

Michael winked at her. "I just want to see how things develop.

Anne was suddenly quite sure that Michael had already discussed the ownership of the vase with Hal as well, and that he had already known Anne's position. "So what about this ownership question? What do I do? I don't really want to be the victim here."

Michael shrugged. "I don't think you need to do anything, at least not yet. A crime appears to have been committed, and that's enough for me to get to work. The real significance of the ownership question is going to come up if there's an insurance claim or a civil suit of some sort. And at that point, the question of who actually owned the vase at the time it was stolen will probably have to be decided by a court."

Anne's heart sank at these words, though she took some hope from the fact that it was not an immediate issue. Perhaps it would never need to be settled.

"But as for being a victim, Anne, consider this. It was well known that the proceeds from the sale of the vase were to go to the library. So in stealing the vase, somebody has arguably dealt the library a serious blow by depriving it of that donation. It's possible that whoever stole the vase did so because they wanted to hurt you or the library."

* * *

Anne slept poorly that night. She stared up into the darkness, berating herself. She knew from the start that the vase would be trouble. She hadn't listened to her own reservations and had instead allowed her friends to talk her out of her misgivings. She should not have overlooked the warning sign of the donor's anonymity.

Clearly, she'd been motivated by greed for the large sum of money that would come to the library.

At that point, even Anne could recognize that her self-reproach had gone beyond reasonable. Whatever the nature of her conflicted feelings about the donation had been, she knew perfectly well that greed had not been a factor. Anne said a prayer for peace of mind and finally dropped off to sleep.

The next day Anne didn't necessarily feel refreshed after her long night, but her head was clearer. What she needed was a new project. She recalled her promises to Wendy to dig out Aunt Edie's matryoshka dolls and the book she'd written about them.

Anne had a vague recollection of packing away a box marked *mat. dolls* in the attic during the library's renovation, but that was such a chaotic period that she still hadn't found everything that had been relocated.

The opportunity to have the dolls appraised, however, was enough motivation to tackle the jumbled labyrinth of the attic. She didn't necessarily expect that they were worth much money, but she wanted to know more about the culture that existed around collecting them. It had been years since she read Aunt Edie's book, but she remembered that her aunt had focused on the history and cultural significance of the dolls in Russia, and she had devoted little or no space to their status as collectibles in America.

Really, Anne thought, she should read Aunt Edie's book again anyway. She was surprised at how close she had come to forgetting about it entirely.

She smiled as she recalled her years in college and her early time as a librarian. Back then, whenever she visited an unfamiliar library, she had always checked to see if they had a copy of Aunt Edie's book in their collection. Of course, they almost never did—it was a specialized book on a narrow topic that had been given limited circulation. But every once in a while, she would find it listed and it gave her a thrill.

The first couple of times it had happened, she called Aunt Edie to tell her about it. Her aunt was pleased, of course, but really, she would say, she was much more interested in hearing about what Anne was up to.

It occurred to Anne that she now had a library of her own. She should have Aunt Edie's book in her own collection! And it was the work of a local author, to boot. She could kick herself for never having thought of it before. She definitely needed to get hold of some additional copies. If she didn't have more than one upstairs, she could probably find a copy or two online from used book dealers. In fact, she could use the dolls and the book together for a display.

While this thought pleased her, it also reminded her that she had yet to begin a new display for the Children's Room. She had recently read a new biography of Martin Luther King Jr. written for young adults, and she had some ideas for building a display around it.

But first things first, she told herself.

Two hours later, she was still rooting around in the attic. As usual, she had found herself all too easily distracted by things she was *not* looking for. This made for pleasant trips down memory lane but kept her from accomplishing her task. At least the search had taken her mind off that stolen vase for a while.

At last, she uncovered a box labeled *mat. dolls*. In fact, it turned out there were two boxes of dolls. She decided to remove herself from other temptations and carried them down into the living room before opening them.

The dolls were, she was pleased to find, as beautiful as she remembered. Aunt Edie had brought them back from Russia decades ago, when she was working as a travel writer. Although Anne now suspected the reason for Aunt Edie's trip may have had secret motivations as well. They would likely never know the extent of her clandestine escapades. Aunt Edie had packed the dolls carefully, wrapped in old towels. There were five sets in all, but one of them went up to an especially large size and consisted of a dozen finely made dolls. The outermost doll was a peasant grandmother in a headscarf, holding a chicken in her arms. Just underneath her was a woman with black hair showing around her headscarf. She held a basket of bread. The rest of the dolls were of children, with the last being a cheery-faced infant swaddled in bright red. This was not one of the sets that stood out in Anne's memory, though she recalled it as soon as she saw it.

Inside one of the boxes, she also found a copy of Aunt Edie's book, rubber-banded together with a large manila envelope. It must have been her own copy, Anne thought, or at least one of them. Anne knew that her copy was packed away elsewhere. That was good—it meant that she had at least two copies in hand already.

The old rubber band broke when she tried to remove it. She unclasped the flap of the envelope and peered inside. The envelope was stuffed with old newspaper clippings. Perhaps they were reviews of the book, though it seemed odd that such a specialized book should receive so much attention from the press.

She closed the envelope and set it aside to examine when she had more time. She needed to get downstairs to relieve Remi Miller so the young woman could get some lunch. But first, Anne quickly looked through the copy of her aunt's book. She checked the title page to see if this copy had been inscribed to anyone, but it had not. When she flipped through the pages, she found that they were marked and annotated, some lightly and some heavily. Reading a few, she realized that they appeared to be notes and edits toward a revised version of the book.

Anne smiled, pleased by this evidence that Aunt Edie had kept up her interest in the dolls, at least for a time. She would treasure this as her aunt's working copy and find some others to add to the collection. Since the book was out of print, she'd have to be creative in acquiring more copies, but she had a few tricks up her sleeve.

For now, she had to set all this aside and get back to the business of running a library.

Chapter Five

That afternoon, Anne sat at the checkout desk, searching online for ideas and images to go with her planned display around the Martin Luther King Jr. biography. She was so intent that she hadn't noticed the sound of the door opening, so she was surprised when a voice nearby said, "After what happened the last time, I thought I'd better come down."

Anne looked up and smiled to see her friend Grace Hawkins, editor of the *Blue Hill Gazette*. As much as she liked Grace, Anne had been unable to hide her dismay at the paper's story about the donation of the vase. Grace had gently reminded Anne that she'd tried to contact her about the story, but Anne hadn't return the call. Nevertheless, Anne could tell that Grace regretted upsetting her friend. Now Grace's face showed a mixture of anxiety and determination.

Anne blinked once and her smile faded a degree. "I take it this isn't a social call?"

"You realize that I can't just ignore the theft of the vase. It's a news story. Half the town is talking about it already." Grace shrugged. "It's my job."

Anne gave a slow nod. "Yes, I know."

"You don't have to give me a quote, of course, but I hope you will. The donation of the vase was intended to benefit the library, so that's necessarily part of the story. It would be appropriate to have a reaction from you."

"And if I don't give a quote, will the story say that I had 'no comment'?" Anne immediately regretted her confrontational tone.

But Grace was accustomed to such responses and took it in stride. "No, I won't do that. But if there's no quote from you in the story, you'll just have that many more people coming in to ask you about it in person."

Anne could appreciate this point, since she'd already had a number of patrons asking about the theft. "Well, it's already a topic of general conversation, but I agree, I should probably say something." She looked up at her friend. "I'm just not sure what. I've already told you that I had mixed feelings about the donation to begin with." And then, alarmed, she added quickly, "Not that I want that..."

"I know, I know," Grace reassured her. "That's off the record. I'll tell you what—I can give you until five today, if you think you can call me with something by then. Would that work?"

"Thank you, Grace. Yes, I promise to call you before then." Anne gave a faint smile. "I guess for you it's pretty exciting, huh? Big story?"

Grace grinned. "The theft of a ten-thousand-dollar vase? Given by an anonymous donor? Replaced in its cabinet by a mysterious fake? Oh yeah." She winked and headed out the door.

* * *

Anne had been brooding over her quote for about twenty minutes, drafting out different options on a pad of paper, when

Wendy Pyle threw open the door, crouched while glancing furtively about, and then sidled up to the checkout desk.

"Watch out for me," she announced in a hushed tone. "I am a *suspect.*"

"What?" Anne exclaimed.

Wendy straightened up and laughed. "Oh yes. I had a call this morning from your friend Officer Banks. He wanted to schedule a time for me to go down to the station and be interviewed. I said, 'You'll never take me alive, copper.'"

Anne gave her a skeptical look.

"Well, okay, I actually said I'd be down there at five."

"But why?"

"They're talking to everyone on the committee," Wendy said. "The vase disappeared sometime between Saturday and Monday, right? Well, we had a committee meeting at the museum Saturday night." She shrugged. "We might be able to shed some light, as they say."

"I'm not sure that raises you to the level of suspect."

"Probably not, no." Wendy feigned disappointment. "What about 'person of interest'? I always thought that sounded glamorous."

As she spoke, Alex Ochs entered the library and approached.

"Speaking of suspicious characters…," Wendy added.

"No one in his right mind would deny that you are a person of interest, Wendy," said Alex.

"Why thank you, sir," she responded with a curtsy. "And what about you? Have you had your grilling yet?"

Alex nodded. "Oh yes, thoroughly grilled, as of this morning. I had to give you up."

"Curses," said Wendy. "Now I'll have to go on the lam."

"Oh, no you don't," Anne said. "You're not going anywhere. You have six library books checked out!" They all laughed, and then Anne said, "Well, it certainly sounds like they're being very thorough."

"Oh yes," Wendy agreed. "They've talked to everyone who works or volunteers for the museum and everyone who works with Miles Bridges. They're even trying to track down everyone who visited the museum on Saturday and Monday, but of course, the museum doesn't keep track of the names of visitors. Still, they're trying."

"Have you talked to them yet?" Alex asked Wendy, and when she shook her head, he continued, "Well, you can laugh about being grilled, but they were actually pretty darn thorough. I had to tell them not only about the meeting on Saturday, but I also had to account for my whereabouts for the entire weekend."

"I thought Banks was your old friend?" Wendy asked, looking back and forth between Alex and Anne. "Didn't you all go to high school together?"

"Even so," Alex said, "he was determined to extract every bit of information that he could."

Anne looked at him sharply. "Why? What happened?"

Alex glanced down, a sheepish expression on his face. "Well, I had to tell him about everything I did on Saturday."

The women watched him expectantly.

"I'm a little behind on this house I'm building, and I went to the site by myself to catch up a bit. And I was using the nail gun, and, well, maybe rushing a little bit, and I got careless and . . . nailed part of my jeans to a stud."

"Your jeans!" Anne exclaimed. "Alex, you could have put that nail right into your leg."

"Well, I didn't," he said quickly. "But the thing was, the way that the nail was placed limited my movement. I couldn't get the leverage to pull myself free, the denim wouldn't tear, and I couldn't reach for another tool to free myself. So I had to call one of my workers to come out and help me. I ended up waiting for him for almost an hour. That's why I was late for the meeting," he added to Wendy.

The two women glanced at each other and struggled not to laugh.

"So did you explain all this to Michael?" Anne asked. When Alex nodded, she added, "What did he say?"

"He said it was a good thing I had someone who could corroborate such a story," he admitted, causing both women to finally break down laughing. "But he was just teasing me," he added plaintively.

After they had finished laughing, the conversation returned to the theft of the vase and the police investigation.

"Have you heard whether the police have been able to talk with the donor yet?" Anne asked, but neither Wendy nor Alex knew anything. Glancing down at her desk, Anne said, "And now I have this to worry about too." She gestured to the pad of paper she'd been writing on. "I need to provide a quote to Grace Hawkins for her story about the theft, and I need to do it this afternoon. I just don't want to sound like the library was the owner of the vase. It wasn't."

Alex gave her a puzzled look. "Why does it matter?"

"Michael was talking to me about insurance claims and civil suits. I can't allow the library to be exposed to that kind of liability."

Wendy, who had traveled this terrain with Anne several times, said, "I think your quote should be an expression of sympathy."

"Sympathy?"

"Sure, sympathy for the donor, who wanted to do something good for the library and whose intent has now been thwarted. And sympathy for the patrons of the library, who now will not be able to benefit from the benefactor's generosity."

A smile of relief spread across Anne's face. "Yes," she said. "Yes, that's it exactly."

* * *

"Wendy gave you good advice," Anne's father said.

"Yes," said Anne, "I thought so. I had to get the quote to the paper before five o'clock, so that's what I went with. But I'm glad to hear you think it was good too."

Once she had gotten Ben and Liddie settled down to a board game after dinner that evening, Anne had called her folks in Florida to bring them up-to-date on events in Blue Hill.

"But did you say that Alex is a suspect, dear?" Her mother's voice, on their other extension, sounded concerned.

"No, not a suspect, Mom. The police are interviewing everyone on the planning committee."

"But you said he had to account for his movements for the entire weekend."

"I think that's just the police being thorough."

"That Alex is such a nice man..." Her mother sighed.

Anne could hear the unspoken conclusion to her mother's sentence. Since Anne had returned to Blue Hill, her mother had occasionally hinted about her hopes that Anne and Alex might resume their high school romance. Her parents had loved her husband, Eric, dearly, but they also wanted their daughter to find happiness again now that Eric was gone.

Anne knew that her mother meant no slight to Eric when she said such things, but these comments still caused the pain of her loss to flare up again in her heart. As usual, she simply ignored the remark.

"So," she said to change the subject, "guess what I dug out of the attic today. Aunt Edie's matryoshka dolls!"

"Oh yes, the dolls!" her mother exclaimed. "You always loved those when you were a girl. She had a wonderful collection, didn't she?"

"Are you going to have them appraised?" asked her father, and Anne smiled. The two of them thought a lot alike.

"I thought I would," she admitted. "I don't think they're really all that valuable, but it would be interesting to hear an expert talk about them."

"You never know," said her father.

"I also found a copy of the book Aunt Edie wrote about them."

Her father chuckled. "Ah yes, the infamous book."

"Infamous?" Anne was startled. "Why infamous?"

"Well, you know, there was that whole business in the newspaper..." His voice trailed off.

"What are you talking about?"

"She won't remember that, Dale," Anne's mother said. "That was before she was born."

"So tell me about it," Anne demanded.

"Well...," her father began and then was silent for several long moments. "Okay," he finally admitted, "I really don't remember the details. I've just always associated that book with some kind of controversy. Do you remember, Charlene?"

"No, I'm sorry, dear. I really don't."

But her father's earlier mention of the newspaper had reminded Anne of the envelope full of clippings that she'd found with the book. Perhaps there would be an answer there.

While she mulled that over, her father reverted to the earlier topic. "I hope the police keep you up-to-date on the investigation," he said. "I want to hear all about it. Who knows, perhaps *you'll* be able to help solve the mystery of the missing vase." Her father made a running joke of Anne's propensity for clearing up little puzzles.

"Bite your tongue," Anne exclaimed. "With this liability business hanging over my head, I'm staying as far away from that investigation as possible."

* * *

When Anne got off the phone, it was time to put the kids to bed. They were more reluctant than usual, and by the time she finally had them settled, she was more than ready for bed herself.

But her curiosity wouldn't allow her to sleep without first taking at least a quick look at those newspaper clippings to see if she could discover the nature of the "controversy" that her father had mentioned.

Sitting at the kitchen table, she upended the envelope and spilled the clippings out onto the tabletop. As she had suspected, a couple were reviews of the book, clipped from glossy, specialized magazines. She noted with pleasure that these were full of praise for Aunt Edie's work.

But most of the clippings appeared to come from newspapers, specifically from the *Blue Hill Gazette*. One was a lengthy feature article about Aunt Edie and the book, the kind of thing you would expect a small-town paper to run about a local author. But the rest appeared to chronicle a lengthy exchange in the letters column.

The clippings were all dated, and the first had appeared a week after the feature story. It was signed by "Patrick Henry," which Anne immediately suspected was a pseudonym. As she read the letter, she was astonished to find her beloved aunt accused of being a communist sympathizer and Soviet propagandist.

She laughed out loud at the thought.

This Patrick Henry apparently believed that any work sympathetic to any aspect of Russian culture or history must be part of an effort to "lull Americans into a sense of complacency," as he put it, regarding what he called the "Soviet threat." Matryoshka dolls were the product of Russian culture, Russian culture had given rise to Soviet-style communism, so following that logic, such dolls were somehow implicated in communism's development, and any admiration of them must be an attempt to promote Soviet ideology.

The misguided logic nearly took Anne's breath away.

Aunt Edie's book had been published in 1965, which Anne knew to be several years after the height of McCarthyism and the Red Scare. But even if the tide of anticommunist hysteria was receding by then, she reflected, people didn't change their opinions overnight. She imagined there were still plenty of people well into the following decade who still clung to some of the crazier notions of the fifties.

However, it was one thing to consider such possibilities in the abstract and quite another to see the proof of it in black and white—and directed against her blameless and beloved aunt Edie.

Anne sat at the table and stared off into space. How did one deal with such blind fanaticism?

The thought saddened her and she felt suddenly exhausted. She stuffed the clippings back into the envelope, telling herself she'd finish reading them another time, and went to bed.

Chapter Six

The next morning, Anne was still feeling subdued. The new edition of the *Gazette* was out, and the paper once again featured its photograph of the vase on the front page. The story the picture illustrated this time, however, was very different.

Reading through it, Anne was satisfied with the quote she had given to Grace. She was lucky to have a friend like Wendy. Anne was also interested to note that Miles Bridges was, for the time being, still withholding the identity of the anonymous donor, though the implication seemed to be that this information had been shared with the police. Anne wondered who the donor was and if she would ever know now that the vase was gone.

About midmorning, Grace Hawkins called to see what Anne had thought of the story.

"It's great," Anne said, meaning it. "Thank you so much."

"I didn't want to bring this up yesterday," Grace said, "but I do have something I'd like to discuss with you. How would you feel about meeting for lunch?"

Intrigued, Anne agreed.

* * *

Anne arrived at the Keystone Café to find Grace already waiting for her. She was in a good mood and didn't seem interested in talking about the missing vase, for which Anne was grateful.

They each ordered salads, and as they ate, Anne told Grace about her aunt's book and the clippings she had found that related to it. When they reached their coffee, Grace finally seemed ready to broach her topic.

"I'm glad to hear that my predecessors at the *Gazette* did a good job on the feature about your aunt," she said. "Writing about books and authors is an important part of a newspaper's job, don't you think?"

"Oh yes," Anne replied, sipping her coffee. "The book review is still my favorite section of the *New York Times*. It's a shame, though. Most newspapers have cut way back on the number of book reviews they run. Aside from the *Times*, there aren't many left that still have a separate book review section." She gave an apologetic smile and shrugged. "I take a professional interest in book journalism."

Grace nodded. "One of my goals for a while now has been to get more coverage of books into the *Gazette*. Maybe a regular column."

Anne looked up with shining eyes. "Oh, Grace, I think that would be wonderful! I'd love to see more discussion of books on the local level."

Grace smiled like a hunter who had successfully sprung a trap. "I'm glad to hear you say that, Anne, because I was hoping that you would agree to write it."

Anne froze with her coffee mug in midair. "Me?" She could hear the alarm in her own voice.

"You'd be wonderful at it, Anne," Grace said quickly. "I've seen you at the library. You're always recommending books to people, telling them why they'll like something. Writing a column would be exactly what you do every day, just in a slightly different format."

Anne blinked and set down her mug. "But that's just talking with people, Grace. Conversation. Writing something for publication is a very different thing. Besides, when I'm in the library, I'm recommending books to people based on what I already know about their tastes. Writing for the paper would be like…talking into the void with no feedback. Without some sort of context, how would I decide what to write about? What if I couldn't keep coming up with new topics in time for your deadlines?"

Grace laughed. "As for feedback, I doubt there will be any shortage of that. And when it comes to topics, well, I still say it's just what you do every day. I've never seen you at a loss to talk about books. New books are being published all the time. I don't see how you could have a shortage of material. But I'll tell you what, we could start by making it a monthly column. That way, the deadlines would not come around too quickly. And if you find you like it, there would always be the opportunity to run it more frequently."

Anne knew her doubt and hesitation still showed on her face.

"Don't feel you have to answer now. Just think about it, okay?"

Anne nodded in relief. "Okay."

"Oh, one more thing." Grace spoke with the tone of someone who has forgotten to mention something significant. "You understand that, well, our freelance rates aren't great, right?"

Grace seemed worried that this might be the deal-breaker, but Anne smiled reassuringly. "Oh no, I assumed that would be the case. No, the thing that tempts me—and yes, I am tempted—is the chance to talk about books and promote the library." After a moment, she added in a firm voice, "I'll think about it."

* * *

"Is there something wrong, dear? You're awfully distracted."

Anne's head snapped up and she saw Mildred Farley gazing at her with concern. "Mildred! I'm so sorry. No, nothing's wrong. I was just thinking about something."

The older woman nodded and sat in a nearby chair. "Would you like to talk about it?" Mildred had been one of Aunt Edie's closest friends, and she had taken a protective interest in Anne ever since she had returned to Blue Hill to run the library. "Is it about this vase business?"

Anne smiled ruefully. "No, not that. It's nothing important. I just can't make up my mind about something." She paused and then explained, "Grace Hawkins has asked me to write a column about books for the *Gazette*, and I can't decide whether I want to do it or not."

"But that's a marvelous idea," Mildred said. "You'd be wonderful."

Anne smiled. Mildred's automatic and whole-hearted support was exactly the reaction that Aunt Edie would have given. But that didn't mean Mildred was correct. "Thank you, but I'm not quite as confident as you are. Grace says that it would be just like recommending books to people here at the library, but I'm not so sure. A newspaper reaches an awful lot of people. How am I going to find books month after month that will appeal to everyone?"

"You won't, dear. Of course you won't." Mildred shook her head slowly. "But that's not the point, is it? Your job isn't to find books that will appeal to every taste. That's not possible. Your job would simply be to find interesting books and tell people what makes them worthwhile. It's up to them to decide if the book appeals to them. And if it doesn't, well, there's always next time." She paused as she considered this, and then added, "Of course, you'd have to cover a decent variety, not the same kind of book over and over. But as long as you do that, then I would say that you've done your job."

It seemed obvious when Mildred said it like that, but Anne had been so hung up on the idea that she could only write about books with mass appeal that these words came as a revelation.

She nodded, frowning in thought as a memory surfaced. She recalled her late husband, Eric, finally putting down the Sunday *New York Times* sometime in the middle of the afternoon. He told her that he enjoyed reading the reviews of the books that he would never get to himself, or that he would never even want to read. "A well-written review gives you a glimpse of a part of the world you might never otherwise know," he'd said.

"It's such a shame about the vase," Mildred said after a moment. "It would have been such a boon for the library. You must be so disappointed."

Anne shrugged. "To tell you the truth, it all seems a little unreal. We never had the money to begin with, so it's hard to feel like we've lost something. And Aunt Edie left the library pretty well funded."

Mildred nodded. "She did. Edie thought it all out very carefully before she made her will. But it never hurts to have a bit more in the bank." She stood up again and laid a consoling hand on Anne's arm. "I'm sure you'll figure it out." She started to step away.

"Figure what out?" Anne asked, thinking Mildred was overestimating the blow to the library's finances.

"Why, who stole the vase, of course. Bye now!"

Anne watched her go. Her fondness for the elderly lady prevented her from disagreeing, but she still wondered why everyone thought it was up to her to do the police's work for them.

* * *

Wendy called that evening, and Anne was surprised to hear a note of strain and worry in her voice. "Could I come over and talk? Would that be all right?"

The kids were done with their dinner and settled in front of the television by the time Wendy arrived. Anne sat at the kitchen table, bursting with curiosity and concern.

"It's about that vase," Wendy said, and Anne's heart sank. She was sick of this topic.

"What about it?"

"I just..." Wendy stopped in exasperation. "It sounds so silly and petty, but it's really bothering me."

"What is?"

"You know how the police talked to all of the members of the Railroad Days committee as part of their investigation?"

Anne nodded.

"I found out that all the other members of the committee have been told that they've been 'cleared' by the investigation. Not that, you know, it's a big official thing, but the police have said something like that to every member of the committee. Except me."

Anne raised her eyebrows, waiting for her friend to continue.

"So I thought, you know, I'd call up your friend Officer Banks and say, 'Hey, how come I haven't been cleared? Everybody else has.' So I called him up, and he said he couldn't say that I *was* cleared. So I said, 'Am I a suspect?' And he said something about it not being that cut-and-dried, and he danced around the question a bit more, but the bottom line is that yes, apparently I am a suspect!" Wendy's voice rose on the final words in a combination of indignation and distress. "Can you believe it?" She gave a quavering laugh and reached out an unsteady hand for her mug of tea.

Anne decided her best course was to remain calm and practical. "But that makes no sense. Why should the other committee members be cleared and not you?" She recalled what Wendy had told her earlier. "You were all there together for a meeting, right? That Saturday night? If one of you has been cleared, you should all be cleared. You were all together."

The unhappiness showed plainly on Wendy's face. "Well, that's the thing," she said in a more subdued tone. "We weren't all together for the whole time. I went back after the meeting." She looked up at Anne and shrugged. "I forgot my phone."

"I see," Anne said slowly. "So because you went back when the others weren't there, you don't have the full alibi that the rest of them do."

Wendy nodded.

"Did anyone see you?"

"Yes, but that just makes it worse. One of the extra security guards saw me as I was leaving. They're there twenty-four-seven now, and he's on the weekend shift. *But* he wasn't with me the whole time I was there. So I could have taken the vase before he saw me."

"I see." Anne thought for a few moments. "But still, Wendy, just because the police can't say you're completely in the clear, that can't be the same thing as being an actual suspect. I'm sure they don't really think you stole the vase. This business about not being cleared is just a technicality, surely."

A faint line of tears shimmered in Wendy's eyes. "Yes, that's more or less what Officer Banks said. I mean, he wasn't quite so definitive about it, but that was the idea he was getting at."

"Well there you go, then."

"Yes, but they don't have any other suspects, do they?" Wendy said sharply. "They may not consider me a very serious suspect, but that doesn't mean they have a better one. As far as I can tell, I'm the *only* one. And so the only suspect must necessarily be the strongest one they've got."

"They're not going to charge you just because they don't have anyone else." Anne spoke strongly, but the look on Wendy's face told her that this was exactly what her friend feared. "Just because you went back into the museum, that's not enough to make you the thief. I mean, they have to build a case, they have to be able to prove something in order to charge someone. And I'm sure that they are clear in their own minds that you *didn't* do it.'"

Though Wendy looked slightly reassured, Anne could tell that her friend had already been over this ground in her own mind.

"Besides," Anne continued as a fresh thought struck her, "you don't know that you're the only suspect. You don't know what the police have turned up in their investigation. It's not like they're going to tell you everything they've learned. For all you know, they have other stronger suspects."

Wendy shook her head doubtfully. "Banks didn't say anything like that."

Anne thought back to the afternoon when the theft was discovered and how even at the very beginning of the investigation, Michael Banks was not letting on about everything he knew. "I wouldn't read too much into that," she said. "I think that the police have to be very discreet while investigating a case."

At that, Wendy finally began to look a bit more hopeful—but when Wendy left half an hour later, Anne could tell she was still worried.

Chapter Seven

Anne slept fitfully that night. She awoke before dawn, and as she listened to the distant crowing of a rooster, she pieced together the strands of the nightmare she'd had.

The vase had been put on display in the Blue Hill Library despite her protests. Once it was set up, it kept growing and growing, until Anne had to squeeze around it just to do her work. On top of that, people kept piling into the library to see the vase. It was hot and cramped, not to mention dangerous. She tried to shout above the crowd that everyone should form a line, but she kept getting shoved farther back until she was against the wall. Finally, the crowd tipped the vase over and it shattered with a horrendous crash. Only then did the crowd disperse, and Anne was left staring down at a million tiny shards of ancient pottery.

The dream had been so vivid that Anne caught herself tiptoeing around that morning, afraid she'd step on a piece of the vase. She didn't put much stock in dream symbols or messages, but she knew the nightmare was a manifestation of her worry over Wendy. Though Anne had been quick to downplay Wendy's fears, she had to admit that her friend's behavior looked suspicious.

Anne didn't doubt Wendy was innocent, of course, and she felt fairly confident that Michael Banks would get to the bottom of the mystery. But until then, she could understand why Michael was unable to "clear" Wendy of suspicion in the way she wanted.

Anne knew Wendy well enough to know this would continue to gnaw at her friend.

Anne sat at her desk and fretted, allowing Bella and Remi Miller to do the bulk of the morning's work. She didn't even respond when the phone rang. Remi stole to the desk and picked it up. Anne realized with a slight jolt that the sisters had been creeping about quietly all morning, apparently afraid of disturbing her. Impatient with herself, Anne looked up to see Remi holding the handset to her chest.

"It's the police," Remi whispered, her eyes wide.

"Oh, good!" Anne exclaimed to her assistant's confusion. Anne accepted the receiver and said, "Hello?"

Just as she'd hoped, it was Michael Banks. "How are you, Anne? Everything okay?"

"Yes, I'm fine. Do you have some news?"

"Not news, I'm afraid, no. But I was hoping that you could come down to the station and give a more complete statement than you had time for the other night."

Though somewhat disappointed, Anne saw a chance to quiz Michael about Wendy's status in the investigation. "Yes, of course, I'd be happy to."

"That's great. This afternoon, do you think? Maybe about..."

Anne interrupted him. "I could come right now."

After another slight hesitation, Michael said, "That would work too. I'll...I guess I'll see you in a few minutes, then."

Anne hung up and quickly began gathering her purse and sweater. "Remi, I have to go down to the police station. You and Bella will have to hold the fort while I'm gone." She glanced up to see Remi give a nervous nod. "It's okay. I just need to talk with them about this vase business." Stepping around the desk, she moved toward the door, turning her head to continue talking to Remi. "There's plenty of shelving to be done, though one of you will have to be sure to man the desk. I shouldn't be gone too..."

As she reached for the door, it opened from the other side and Reverend Tom appeared smack in her path.

Though Anne tried to stop, she had too much momentum and she walked right into him, spilling a load of books from his arms. Remi let out a little screech.

"Oh, Reverend Tom! I'm so sorry!" Anne exclaimed, feeling unusually flustered. She tried to help him retrieve the books but only succeeded in getting in his way.

After a moment, the pastor straightened and said, "No harm done, Anne, no harm done. And these books look no worse for the wear." He cast an appraising eye over them, then looked back at her. "But don't let me keep you, if you're in a hurry."

"I'm going down to the police station," Anne explained, gathering her wits again. "They've just called."

Reverend Tom raised his eyebrows. "Is there news?"

"No, no," Anne said, feeling a bit foolish for her hurry. "I just have to...expand on my statement."

The pastor nodded, and Anne, still somewhat embarrassed, was suddenly annoyed all over again by the situation.

"I just knew it," she said to herself as she walked out of the library. "I knew all along that this vase was going to be trouble."

* * *

Fortunately, by the time she reached the station, Anne had calmed down and begun to think about the questions that she wanted to ask. Michael Banks met her at the entrance, led her to a small conference room, and offered her a cup of coffee, which she accepted in order to give herself more time to order her thoughts.

"I'm sorry to have to drag you down here, Anne," Michael said as he opened a folder and shuffled some papers.

"No problem. I'm just as eager to get to the bottom of this as you are."

Michael pulled out a typed version of the statement she had given at the museum, and they spent half an hour reviewing it line by line. Anne added as much detail as she could recall, but she was aware that nothing in her statement was particularly helpful.

When they had been through it all twice, Michael ripped the sheets from his notepad and added them to his folder. "So," he said, "I promised to keep you updated on the progress of the investigation."

Anne straightened in her seat. This was the part she had been waiting for.

Michael spread his hands. "Sadly, there's little to report so far."

Anne could tell from his tone that he would say no more until she had given some sort of response. "Michael, why is Wendy Pyle a suspect?"

If he was surprised by the question, he didn't show it. He gazed at her steadily for a few moments and then said, "If that were true, why would it be of concern to you?"

"Because she's my friend. Because I'm sure she didn't do it. And because I happen to know that she's very upset about being considered a suspect." Anne spoke evenly but with authority in her voice.

Michael did not change his expression. "Anne, despite what I said a moment ago about keeping you up-to-date, I'm sure you can understand that it applies only within certain limits. In an ongoing investigation, there is a great deal of information that we need to keep confidential so as not to jeopardize our inquiries." He paused a moment. "For instance, while I might be able to respond to a general question such as 'Do you have any suspects?', I could not possibly talk with you about specific suspects. Do you see?" He watched her carefully as he spoke.

After a moment's thought, Anne said, "Do you have any suspects?"

Michael gave her a quick smile. "Unfortunately, none that are really viable."

Anne felt a rush of relief, though she could understand why Wendy would find such an oblique hint unsatisfying. Knowing she would get no further information out of Michael on this topic, at least for the time being, Anne moved on to her next question. "What about the donor, then? Have you been in touch with him…or her?"

Michael pursed his lips. "We have not talked with the donor—yet. Miles Bridges is arranging to bring the donor down here to the station."

Something in his tone caught her attention. "That…seems very helpful of him," she offered. "Has he also been helpful with the replacement vase?"

"Mr. Bridges is nothing if not helpful," Michael muttered, and then a quick look of regret came over his face. Anne thought he'd let something slip, but he clearly wasn't going to compound his mistake by saying so.

"Michael, am I going to find out who this mysterious donor is? I think I have a right to know, especially if there are issues about ownership and insurance claims, like you mentioned the other day. I feel like the library is exposed to possible liability, and yet I know almost nothing about the whole situation, about who donated the vase or why, or what their expectations were, or what they think about the fact that it's been stolen." She stopped abruptly, afraid that she had started to ramble.

After a moment, Michael nodded. "I'm not prepared—yet—to give you that information on my own authority, but you make good points and I promise to bring that all up with the donor when I have a chance to talk with them. Will that do for now?"

"Thank you, Michael," she said with feeling. "Thank you very much."

* * *

Anne left the police station reassured that she'd have more information soon but unsure if Michael's vague statement regarding suspects would ease Wendy's mind. She also thought it odd that Miles Bridges found it necessary to escort the donor of the vase to the police station.

In her mind, Anne pictured a wealthy, pampered dowager being driven in a black Rolls Royce by a chauffeur whose black suit and hat complemented the car. Why couldn't she come by herself? Wouldn't Michael feel that Miles was exerting undue influence on her testimony to the police?

Anne wondered about the extent of Miles's interest and if she might talk to him herself, perhaps at his antiques shop. That would give her a chance to get a better look at his operation too, and see for herself how appraisals were done.

She nodded, feeling better now that she had some course of action. She'd put Miles on her growing to-do list for the week.

* * *

The next morning, Anne sat behind her desk, still worried about Wendy. She had called her friend the night before and described her interview with Michael Banks in detail, but no matter how confident she made her reassurances sound, it was clear that nothing but an unambiguous statement from the police was going to ease Wendy's mind about her status as a suspect.

Anne hoped that the police would resolve the case quickly for the sake of her friend.

The thing that puzzled Anne the most about the theft was the substitution of the replacement vase. The theory that this was done to delay discovery of the crime didn't make sense to her. After all, the theft would be discovered eventually—at the time of the auction, if not before. Even odder, the replacement vase, though it looked similar, was not a replica of the one that had been stolen.

So what was the value of a decoy that might give the thief only a few days to—what? Leave the area? Find a buyer? It was a lucky break that they had discovered the theft so quickly, and it must be the worst-case scenario from the point of view of the thief, especially if they had hoped to gain some time to find a buyer. Michael hadn't said so, but Anne hoped and assumed that the police were monitoring any auctions or dealers where the vase might turn up.

Anne's thoughts were interrupted by the phone ringing.

"Anne? It's Grace. I hope I'm not calling too early."

"Hi, Grace, no, it's not too early. We rise with the chickens around here," Anne said. "What's on your mind?"

"Well…," Grace sounded a little surprised and paused a moment. Anne wondered if she was calling for another quote.

Theft of the vase was bound to be an ongoing story for the paper, and Anne had even tried to come up with something new to say for a follow-up story. Anne wondered if Grace knew that she had been down to the police station the day before. Was she hoping to get information from Anne about the progress of the investigation?

As Anne was trying to decide how much she could share, Grace continued. "I was calling to follow up on our talk the other day. About the possibility of your writing a column for the *Gazette*?"

"Oh, gosh, the column! I said I'd think about it, didn't I?"

"Yes. Yes, you did." Anne could hear suppressed laughter in Grace's tone, as Anne had clearly not thought about it at all. Wendy's troubles and Anne's trip to the police station had put the column idea out of her mind completely.

"Well," Anne said lamely, "Mildred Farley thinks it's a good idea."

Now Grace did laugh. "Okay, that's one on my side. But listen, Anne, I was thinking afterward that I may have been unclear about what I have in mind. You expressed concern about running out of ideas, but I want you to know that you'd have a lot of latitude. By books, I mean a column broadly about reading, writing, library issues. I know that you always have things to say about literacy issues, for instance. That would be perfectly suitable."

Now it was Anne's turn to laugh. "Thank you, but that almost makes it sound more daunting. A big topic like literacy requires so much more thought and organization and..."

"All of which you are quite capable of, Anne," Grace said. "Besides, I'm not suggesting that you'd say everything there is to be said in a single column. I'm just pointing out that you'd have a great deal of flexibility so running out of topics would be unlikely."

Grace paused, but when Anne didn't offer another objection, she continued. "Look, why don't you try it for a few months to see if you can keep it up? It's summer now, and I'm sure you are anticipating more kids using the library. Perhaps you can start with some suggestions for summer reading?"

Anne's mind flew to the display she was designing around the Martin Luther King Jr. biography. That was one of the books she was hoping to push for summer reading. In fact, she would be setting up the display that weekend.

Suddenly, she had an insight. Every time she created a new display for the library, it would also be a potential topic for a newspaper column. Writing to deadline had felt daunting, but Anne was constantly putting together new displays for both the children and adult sections. Indeed, she had far more ideas for book displays than she could actually create. And all those unused ideas would be suitable for newspaper columns as well. Coming up with material would be a snap.

"All right," Anne said brightly. "Okay. I think I can do this. When would be my first deadline?"

* * *

Anne's design for the display had evolved beyond a straight focus on the King biography to include images and information about the civil rights movement as a whole. She had scoured the Web for images related to the era, the kind of images that had been seared into the minds of her parents' generation but which might be unknown to young people. Images of sit-ins at lunch counters and marchers with linked arms in the streets of Selma, Alabama, of children and adults being blasted with water from fire hoses and of a single little girl being escorted by US Marshals into school. To complement that last photo, she also found Norman Rockwell's famous painting *The Problem We All Live With.*

She had printed these and other pictures and mounted each on construction paper with a caption attached. Then she rounded up a score of books, such as *Free at Last* by Sara Bullard, *Witnesses to Freedom* by Belinda Rochelle, and *The Watsons Go to Birmingham – 1963* by Christopher Paul Curtis. As she and Remi Miller assembled these materials into a display, Anne also began to plan out her first newspaper column.

Anne noticed Remi holding one of the pictures and staring down at it. It showed a white woman holding a large placard declaring integration to be immoral.

"It's hard to believe people could think like this," Remi said, shaking her head.

"It wasn't all that long ago," Anne replied.

"Remi placed the image into the display. "Well, I'm glad things aren't like that anymore."

Anne stopped and looked at her. "You don't think so?" The girl responded with an alarmed look, and Anne gestured toward the picture. "We may not see people holding signs quite like that any longer, but that doesn't mean that we have eradicated racial prejudice from our society."

"But we don't have segregation anymore," Remi objected.

"No," Anne agreed, "at least not legalized segregation. But we have to be alert, especially when we are fearful or feel insecure, that prejudices don't become a legitimate, approved part of our culture again."

Remi's face grew thoughtful, but she said nothing.

Anne had reservations, of course, when she made the decision to return to Blue Hill and fulfill Aunt Edie's dream. But one drawback that had not occurred to her until she arrived was how homogeneous Blue Hill could be. She had always enjoyed the bustling, lively, ethnic diversity of her home in Brooklyn, but she had never appreciated just how much until she returned to the small town of her youth. Nor had it occurred to her, before the move, to worry about her children growing up in such an environment.

She reminded herself that she had also grown up with a lack of cultural and ethnic diversity, and though this had resulted in some surprises when she'd gotten out in the wider world, she didn't think the experience had done her any lasting harm. And wary as she was of television, film, the Internet, and other channels of popular culture, these things offered a picture of a more diverse America than had been the case when she was young.

Still, this was one of the things she most missed about their old life in Brooklyn.

Remi asked, "What would be a good book about…?" She gestured toward the display. "You know, not for kids."

"*Parting the Waters* by Taylor Branch," Anne said. "It was the companion volume to a TV special about the era."

"Do we have it?" Remi asked.

Anne smiled. "Oh yes. Yes, we do."

* * *

Anne spent the rest of the day writing her column. Or rather, rewriting it. The first draft had gone pretty smoothly, and she had been pleased. But as she tried to go about her other work, she kept coming back to the draft, rereading it, and tinkering with it.

Sometimes she would open the file, read the whole thing through, and then change just a single word before saving and closing it again. Once or twice, she went back a few minutes later to change that word back to what it had been.

Then she tried printing it out to see what it looked like on paper and found herself making even more edits. When the sheet became completely unreadable, she realized why people used double-space formatting. She entered her edits, changed the line spacing, and printed it again.

She saved each of her drafts as a new file, so around midafternoon, convinced that she must be making things worse rather than better, she compared her current version to her original draft. She was surprised at how satisfied she felt when she realized that all the tinkering and editing really had improved the column.

Grace had given her a deadline of five p.m., but Anne had promised herself that she would not send it in just under the wire. At four o'clock, she told herself sternly that no further changes were allowed and sent the column off to the paper via e-mail, along with a quick prayer that it would be well received.

Chapter Eight

When Wendy walked into the library on Monday morning, Anne's heart sank. She could tell by the look on her friend's face that she was even more upset than she had been a few days before.

Anne sat her friend down and asked her what was wrong. "Still no luck with the police? No progress over the weekend? It's been a week!"

Wendy shook her head. Her normally stylish black bob hung limply on her head, and she was dressed in loose, dark clothing. She looked like she wanted to crawl into a cave. "No, no change."

Anne peered at her friend. "Has something else happened?"

For a moment, Wendy didn't respond. Then she said, "I got a call from Hal McCollum yesterday. Somehow, they all know that I'm the only member of the committee who hasn't yet been cleared by the police." She paused to clear her throat. "They think it would be best if I resigned from the committee while the investigation is going on."

"Oh, for Pete's sake!" Anne exploded. "That's ridiculous."

Wendy shrugged. "I can see their point. This business with the theft is all anyone's talking about. Everyone on the committee, Hal especially, has worked really hard to make Railroad Days a successful community celebration. But the theft is using up all the oxygen. They're concerned that the positive aspects of the event are going to get lost in all the commotion."

"But you've worked hard too," Anne objected. "Their success is due in no small part to your work." She took a breath and calmed herself before continuing. "Oh, Wendy, I'm sorry you are going through this, really, but I do believe the truth will come out. After all, it's only been a week."

Wendy smiled. "Your faith is always uplifting."

She was about to say something more when they heard the sound of the door opening and turned to face Reverend Tom and his wife, Maggie. Maggie threw open her arms to gather Wendy in a tight hug.

"I know what you're going through, and I want you to know that I have total faith in you," Maggie said, pulling back. "You'll make it through this mess. And Anne here is going to get to the bottom of this puzzle." Over Wendy's shoulder Maggie winked at Anne. "We love you and support you one hundred percent!"

Wendy sniffled then smiled.

As Reverend Tom and Maggie returned their library books and went to browse around the library, Anne noticed that Wendy's hands were shaking as she began to check the books back in.

Anne bit her lip. She had an idea but wasn't sure it would go over well. But when she saw Wendy reach for a tissue and dab her eyes, Anne spoke up.

"I'm in the middle of a project that I could use some help with," she started.

Wendy turned and her eyes brightened. That was Wendy—always eager to help someone out. Anne felt more confident and continued.

"It's those nesting dolls of Aunt Edie's. I'm planning to have them evaluated at the appraisal fair, but I want to come to the table a little more prepared, if you know what I mean. You're such a good researcher, I thought perhaps...?"

"Oh, Anne! I would love a quiet project I can get lost in and a warm cup of tea." Wendy smiled, trying to laugh at herself.

"Done!"

Since Reverend Tom and Maggie were the only ones in the library at the moment, Anne called around the corner that she and Wendy were upstairs, but she would be back down in just a minute. Then she led Wendy to her kitchen table and powered up the laptop while Wendy set the kettle on for hot water.

As Wendy made herself at home, selecting a green mint tea from Anne's substantial collection of tea bags, Anne went to retrieve the dolls and a copy of the book Aunt Edie had written about them.

While Wendy researched the matryoshka dolls, Anne returned to the checkout desk. But even as she answered questions and helped patrons find the books they sought, part of her mind was concerned for her friend. She felt helpless and frustrated at her inability to help Wendy in some substantial way. The police investigation had been going on for a week. Why had they not made more progress? Michael Banks had promised to keep her updated, but she'd heard nothing since she met with him.

Her mind turned again to the mystery donor. Michael had assured her that Miles Bridges was arranging for the donor to talk with the police. Had he done so by now? If not, what was taking so long? Had Michael passed on her desire to also meet the donor?

Maggie Sloan had suggested that Anne herself would somehow solve the puzzle, and for Wendy's sake, Anne wished she could. But what could she do to help the investigation and remove this cloud of suspicion from Wendy? Anne knew she needed to let the police do their job, but she felt that she had to take some action or she would burst from frustration.

She hadn't yet paid that call on Miles Bridges. At the very least, she could ask him to pass along to the donor the same message that she had left with Michael Banks. And in the process, she might learn something that would help Wendy.

She was just beginning to plan when she could make a trip over to Midtown Antiques when Wendy came rushing downstairs.

"These dolls are very interesting," Wendy exclaimed. "I'm glad to have a chance to learn something about them. And I think you may find out that they're worth something."

Anne smiled. "I had always assumed they were some old Russian folk craft. I was surprised to learn from Aunt Edie's book that their origin can be traced to two Russians in 1890."

"The painter and the craftsman," Wendy said, nodding her head. "Though they might have been inspired by a traditional Japanese doll. But you're right, it's interesting that we can point to those two men and say, 'They made the very first set.' Still, the dolls caught on quickly, not just in Russia but as a distinctively Russian product all over the world. And apparently," she added, "they have become quite collectible, at least the older ones."

"That's a subject that Aunt Edie didn't get into," Anne said. "Or maybe back when she wrote the book, they weren't considered all that collectible. She said that production of dolls really declined during the Soviet era because handcrafted goods were discouraged in favor of things that could be mass-produced in factories. She was writing in the early 1960s, and she seemed to think that the era of the nesting doll was over, thanks to Soviet suppression."

"Ah, but since the collapse of the Soviet Union," Wendy said, "interest in the dolls has revived, and the production of high-quality, handcrafted dolls has resumed. And along with that, interest in their history has grown. People never stopped making them altogether. They just had to do it on the sly. The handmade sets from that period can be quite valuable, both because of their quality and scarcity." Wendy gave her an intense look. "I think those are the kind of dolls that Edie brought home. And I think at least one of those sets is even older than the sixties era."

* * *

On Wednesday, Anne eagerly collected the latest edition of the *Gazette* and flipped quickly through it until she found the column she had written. There was a brief head note introducing it as a new feature and welcoming Anne to the paper.

She nervously began reading the column, expecting to be on high alert for every flaw. To her surprise, seeing her words set in the column of print gave her a sense of distance and objectivity.

And she was not displeased.

More importantly, Anne felt that she had stretched herself and grown by trying something new. Growth was part of what made life worth living. God had put mankind on the earth to use the gifts He'd given them, not to stagnate. She had also successfully extended her mission as a librarian to bring books to the attention of readers.

As she went about her duties that morning, Anne developed a list of ideas for future columns and jotted down some notes.

Her list ran to a dozen ideas, and she was writing down some extra notes on the last one when Reverend Tom walked in.

Looking up, she gave him a smile. "Weren't you just here yesterday?"

"I was, yes." He held up a hardbound book. "But I read this years ago, and I only checked it out to refresh my memory about a particular bit. I looked it up last night, so now I can return it."

Anne looked at the book as he handed it over. "*The Memory Palace of Matteo Ricci*," she read. "He was the Jesuit missionary who went to China, right?"

Reverend Tom nodded. "That's right. In the sixteenth century. Remarkable man. And an interesting meeting of two cultures."

"You read a lot of history," Anne observed.

"I find it fascinating," Reverend Tom replied with a smile. "Which was one of the reasons why I enjoyed your column in the paper so much. Congratulations, Anne."

She blushed. "Why, thank you. I enjoyed writing it, though I'd kind of forgotten that other people would actually be reading it." She paused and then asked shyly, "So you liked it?"

Reverend Tom nodded. "I did. I'm always happy to see Dr. King remembered, and the book you wrote about sounds like an excellent introduction to the civil rights era for young people." He shook his head. "It's hard to believe that was fifty years ago now.'"

"I've created a display up in the Children's Room that goes along with the book and the column," Anne said.

"Yes, you mentioned that in the paper. I'll have to go have a look." He paused and then asked, "How is Wendy?"

Anne sighed. "She's holding up as best she can, but she's really upset. She worked very hard on this whole Railroad Days event, you know, and I think the fact that she's been shut out of that is bothering her at least as much as the idea that she might be suspected of the theft." Anne paused. "I can't imagine that anyone would really think she's a suspect, can you?"

Reverend Tom shrugged. "I am constantly amazed at what people are willing to believe, or at least unwilling to disbelieve. And the more scandalous and outlandish the rumor, the more some people will be drawn to it."

"But that's like making a conscious decision to believe the worst about somebody," Anne exclaimed, outraged.

"Well," said Reverend Tom slowly, "I think it has less to do with the subject of the rumor and more to do with a love of drama and excitement, which I think all people have to some extent. When a person is wrongly suspected or accused, their friends know that it can't be true, but anyone else might be tempted to take a 'where there's smoke, there's fire' position. Or at least be more willing to entertain that possibility. And every once in a while, you do hear about some guilty person no one suspected."

Anne grimaced. "Still, I think it would be better if we could start by giving people the benefit of the doubt. 'Do unto others,' right?"

"I agree with you, of course," said Reverend Tom, "but in my business, it pays to try to understand why people behave the way they do. Rather than, you know, the way that I think they ought to." He gave a slight smile. "And in the meantime, we must have faith that Wendy will be cleared. It just may take a little time."

Chapter Nine

The next day, Anne went to Midtown Antiques. She considered calling for an appointment, but that seemed too formal. For some reason, she wanted her visit to appear spontaneous.

Midtown Antiques was a dim warren of aisles crowded with furniture, tools, and a wide variety of bric-a-brac. Though the lighting was poor, the shop felt rich with possibility instead of oppressive. Every time Anne turned a corner, she thought she might stumble upon some unexpected treasure. As she drifted through the store, she couldn't resist picking up and examining all manner of objects, even though she had no intention of buying them. Something about the atmosphere of the shop seemed to bring out the wonder and marvel of everything she encountered.

When she asked a clerk for Miles Bridges, she was directed to the storefront next door, which turned out also to be a part of Midtown Antiques. The shop must have grown and expanded over the years.

The other half of the store was completely different. Rather than the crowded aisles and dim lighting, here everything was carefully displayed. It was still crowded, but the aisles were wider, the light was better, the carpet was plusher, and the sense of chaotic abundance was gone. This shop felt expensive and sophisticated. After so many years of telling her children to put their hands in their pockets whenever they were close to breakable things, Anne followed her own advice.

This time when she asked for Miles Bridges, she was asked to wait while the clerk disappeared into the offices at the back of the shop.

Miles soon appeared, and when he saw who it was, he hurried forward. "Anne, what a nice surprise. What can I do for you?"

Now that she was here, Anne realized that she had given no thought to how to approach her request. "I was wondering if I could speak with you a moment. About the vase."

"Such a terrible thing." Miles gestured back in the direction he'd come. "Why don't we go to my office."

He led her through a suite of offices into one on his left. Miles's office looked more like the older, crowded shop than the modern one they'd just left. A desk and a couple of tables were cluttered with small items of all kinds, and a bookcase overflowed with oversized reference volumes.

The antiques dealer led Anne to a seat before seating himself at his desk. "Now then," he said genially, "how can I help you?"

By this time, Anne had decided on the direct approach. "I understand from the police that you are acting as a sort of intermediary with the donor. And that you're going to arrange an interview with the donor for them. Or perhaps have already done so?"

Miles nodded. "It hasn't happened yet, but yes, I have talked with the donor and convinced the person to come forward and assist the police with their inquiries. In fact, I'll be taking the donor down to the station myself, probably next week." He looked a bit troubled as he added this last part.

Anne frowned. "I don't mean to be blunt, but why is this taking so long? I'd think the police would want to talk with the donor as soon as possible."

Miles sighed. "No, you're right. The police are very impatient. But the donor is quite elderly, you see, and in rather poor health. The donor is also, shall we say, difficult. To tell you the truth, I wish now that I had washed my hands of it. Just given the donor's name and address to the police right at the beginning and let them handle it. But I knew that the donor felt very strongly about maintaining anonymity and so I tried to respect that. Now I'm afraid I'm stuck in the middle. But the donor has definitely agreed to accompany me to the police station sometime next week, and with that promise in hand, the police have agreed to wait. I've made it quite clear that if he tries to back out of this, the police will be contacting him directly."

Anne allowed herself a small smile at Miles's use of the pronoun *he*. This was the first time Miles had slipped and used a masculine pronoun instead of saying *the donor*. So much for her imagined white-haired dowager being chauffeured around Blue Hill.

Miles continued. "I gather that part of the reason for the delay is because of his nephew's schedule. He doesn't have much family, and the nephew is the one he relies on. He lives a couple of hours away and has a life of his own, so we had to wait until he could arrange the time as well."

Anne thought these excuses were still pretty thin when it came to the matter of a police investigation, but if the police themselves were willing to wait, what could she say? But this information didn't seem to bode well for her own request.

"Miles, I've made this request with the police, but I'll put it to you directly as well. Since the library has been dragged into this matter, I would very much like to know the identity of the donor myself. Would you be willing to take this request to him? Just as you've acted as an intermediary for the police."

Miles frowned. "I feel quite certain that he will be... resistant to that."

"Based on his behavior so far, I expect he will," Anne replied. "And I realize that he was acting from generous motives when he donated the vase. But the fact remains that because of the donation, the library now finds itself involved in a crime and a police investigation. And at this point, I just feel that I have a right to more information about what is going on." Anne leaned forward. "I also believe that the police will share the information with me at some point on their own authority. But before we get to that point, wouldn't it be preferable if the donor agreed to do so? It's just not reasonable to think that anonymity can be maintained when the whole thing has become a criminal matter."

Miles slowly nodded. "You make very good points, Anne, and I agree with you. So yes, I am willing to take the matter up with the donor. And as you say, you will probably be able to get the information sooner or later from the police. I think he will understand that, and he will agree. Do you want me to try to arrange a meeting, as I have done with the police?"

Anne hadn't expected that. "Why... why yes, I think that might be a good idea. Thank you."

"I think that now, having agreed to speak with the police, it's likely that he will agree to meet you as well. I will certainly ask and let you know."

"Well, thank you very much," she said again. "I'll look forward to hearing from you." She was rising from her chair when another thought struck her. "By the way, I understand you're also helping the police with that fake vase that was left as a substitute?"

Miles had also risen, but a gleam of enthusiasm appeared in his eye. "Ah, well now that *is* interesting," he said. "As a matter of fact *fake* is not really the appropriate term for it."

Anne gave him a puzzled look. "What do you mean?"

"I mean that the second vase is also a legitimate, antique Chinese vase. Or it appears to be, based on the photographs the police have provided."

"Someone replaced one antique vase with another?" Anne asked. "That seems very odd."

"Oh, it's even odder yet," Miles said. "Our preliminary analysis suggests that the value of the second vase is possibly equal to that of the first."

Anne gaped at him.

"It raises an interesting philosophical question, doesn't it?" Miles asked with a touch of eagerness in his voice. "I mean, if a valuable vase is stolen but an equally valuable one is left in its place, what is the extent of the crime, at least in financial terms?"

"I'm not sure I follow you," said Anne.

"Well, clearly the first vase has been stolen, which is a crime. But as I understand the law, it is the value of the stolen item that determines the category of the offense. Petty larceny, grand larceny, et cetera. Right?"

"I suppose so," Anne said slowly. "What do the police have to say to that?"

"As far as they're concerned, the theft of the one vase and the replacement of the other are unrelated. Theft is theft, and the value of the stolen item determines the nature of the crime. The fact that another vase was left behind, whatever its value, is irrelevant, at least from a prosecutor's point of view. But still, I wonder if a court would take the same view. It can't be a very common occurrence."

"Probably not," Anne agreed. "Is there any way to tell where this second vase came from?"

"Not right now," Miles said. "The police won't allow us to physically examine the vase, and we can only learn so much from photographs. But even if we do get to examine it, there's no guarantee that we'll be able to tell where it came from." He stepped out from behind his desk. "Here, hold on just a moment."

He left the room, and Anne thought she could hear him tapping on another door down the hall. After a moment, he returned, trailed by a young woman dressed in a striking black-and-white suit, with stylish, heavy-framed black glasses.

"Anne, this is Angie Staub, our consulting expert in Asian ceramics. Angie usually comes up once a month from Philadelphia, but lately she's been coming up more often to help with the appraisal fair and auction. Angie, we were just discussing the second vase, the one that was left behind when... when the donated vase was stolen. Anne Gibson runs the library in Blue Hill that would have benefited from the auction of the first vase."

Angie Staub gave Anne a wary look but didn't say anything.

"We were just discussing the surprising value of the second vase," Miles prompted, and Angie looked positively alarmed.

Her glance flickered back and forth between Anne and Miles. "Yes, it was quite surprising."

"So you believe that the replacement vase is as valuable as the one that was stolen?" Anne asked.

Angie turned toward Miles. "Should we be...?"

"Oh yes, it's fine," Miles assured her. "I just told you—her library was the beneficiary for the original vase. Though I suppose," he continued thoughtfully, "there could be a question then of just who the second vase belongs to."

Angie shot Miles a reproachful look, and he looked troubled. "Oh dear, I hope I haven't been indiscreet."

"Surely not," Anne said quickly. "The police have already promised to keep me fully informed about the progress of the investigation, so I'm sure they would have shared this information with me anyway."

Miles looked relieved at this, but Angie still appeared to be unhappy.

"Well, I've taken up enough of your time," Anne said, stepping toward the office door. "Thank you very much for your help, Miles. Nice to meet you, Ms. Staub."

She felt like Angie Staub's eyes were boring holes in her back as she left.

Chapter Ten

During the offertory in church on Sunday, Liddie and her Sunday school class got up to sing "He's Got the Whole World in His Hands," and pantomimed the lyrics. Anne couldn't help smiling during the performance, not only because the children were so charming, but also because Liddie had been so determined to get her motions right that she had practiced it all week.

The song made Anne think about what a year it had been for her children, and how this year in her new school, Liddie especially had matured quite a bit. She was learning to focus on her tasks and take responsibilities—like learning this song for church—more seriously.

Anne was so lost in thought that she sat through the choral response, even though the rest of the congregation was standing. When she stood up abruptly during the last verse, she noticed Reverend Tom quickly looking away, suppressing a little chuckle.

That Sunday's attendance was somewhat diminished as people took advantage of the warm summer weekend, and conversation at the coffee hour afterward naturally turned toward plans for the summer.

Anne chatted with Helen Smith, a member of the church's board, who had a rather far-flung family and would be traveling later in the summer to visit them. "Fortunately, my trip isn't scheduled until late July," she said, "so I'll still be in town for the auction."

Maggie Sloan appeared to pull Helen away on some church business, and Anne turned to find herself facing Gertrude Haines, who had apparently been standing at her elbow. Anne gave the older woman a polite smile.

"So, Anne," Gertrude said, "I read your column in the *Gazette*."

"Oh, thank you!" Anne said, smiling somewhat more warmly. By now she had received a number of compliments on the column, but she still found it odd to receive such recognition.

Her bright response seemed to displease Gertrude, who scowled. "You're going to write a column every month?"

"For as long as the paper will let me!"

"And will it always be about books for young people?"

By now, Gertrude's sour tone and expression were obvious, and Anne wondered what she was getting at. However, she continued to respond in an upbeat manner.

"Oh no. I expect to write about all kinds of books. In fact, I think my next column will be about some new presidential biographies. There have been three published within the last few months, so I thought it would make for a good grouping." She couldn't tell if this answer met with Gertrude's approval or not. "But of course, I expect many of the columns to be about children's books. After all, that's an active section for the library, and I get a lot of questions about books from both kids and their parents."

"I see."

Anne's smile now felt artificial, and she took the opportunity to douse it in a sip of coffee.

"And will there always be a display in connection with these columns?" Gertrude asked.

"There won't always be a display for every column, no," Anne said. "I don't change them that often. Though I imagine that every time I *do* create a new display, the theme will also serve as a subject for a column. That's what happened this time. I was already planning the display around the King biography, and it seemed like a natural subject for the first column."

"I see." Gertrude gazed silently at Anne for a moment as she chewed a bite of her donut. "And how do you determine what's appropriate for the displays in the Children's Room?"

Anne was a bit taken aback by the question. "Appropriate?" she repeated. "The displays all feature books that are specifically intended for children. They're the audience. I read all the books myself, but I haven't yet encountered anything that I thought was inappropriate. Publishers are pretty good at developing the right books for the right audiences."

Gertrude gave another little nod and excused herself, leaving a puzzled Anne to watch her retreating back.

* * *

The summer weekends may have been taking a toll on church attendance, but with schools closed for the summer, the library was unusually full of children. Anne had anticipated this, and fortunately both of the Miller twins were interested in earning some extra money for the summer, so the library was well staffed.

In the midst of the commotion, Anne spotted Mildred Farley as she entered, carrying a large shopping bag.

"Goodness, Mildred," Anne exclaimed, hurrying forward to relieve her of the bag, "what have you got there?"

"Do take care, dear," Mildred said, reluctantly releasing the bag. "It's a bit fragile. Just set it on the desk, will you?"

The bag was heavier than Anne expected, and she lowered it gently to the desktop and then stepped back. Mildred waved for her to go ahead, so Anne stepped up to the bag and peered inside it.

"What on earth?" She reached into the bag and slowly pulled out the single object it contained. "A ceramic railroad car?"

"A caboose!" Mildred announced proudly.

"It's fabulous." Anne looked at it from various angles. It was a little larger than a loaf of bread. "Look at the detail in that painting." She set the caboose on the desk. "Have you brought this out for Railroad Days?"

Mildred nodded. "I thought I would donate it to the auction. It was a present from my aunt when I graduated from college." She chuckled. "I've had it for a long time, but it's just been gathering dust in the guest room upstairs, and I thought someone else might appreciate it more than I do. And it seemed appropriate to the theme, don't you think?"

"Absolutely," Anne agreed. "But don't you want to have it appraised before you decide whether or not to donate it?"

Mildred shook her head. "No, no. Let somebody else enjoy it. And if it's worth something, well, more power to them. Besides," she added in a more confidential tone, "I have some other things that I want appraised. I've already signed up for one of the slots."

Mildred was shrewd, and Anne suspected that whatever she had picked out for appraisal would have value. "May I ask what?"

"Of course. I have some lovely pieces of old Zanesville pottery. It's rather collectible these days."

"Oh, I think it is," said Anne. "Shall we see if we can find some information about it?"

Together they did some research both in the library's reference books and online. Anne even found a picture of an umbrella stand that Mildred said looked very much like hers, but they couldn't find any information on current prices for such items.

"Well, that's what the appraisal is for," Mildred said, "though I hope they'll be able to tell me other things as well. It was when I was thinking about those pieces that I suddenly remembered that old ceramic caboose. That's how I got the idea to donate the caboose to the auction."

"Perhaps the museum will want to keep it themselves," Anne suggested.

Mildred shrugged. "That's up to them. "Once I donate it, I don't care what becomes of it. But now, my dear, how are you? And how is your friend Wendy? I hear such things about her."

Anne looked at her in dismay. "What things?"

"Oh well, I don't pay attention to rumors," Mildred said quickly, "but there *are* some people in town who think she may have had something to do with the theft of that vase."

Mildred spoke like someone reluctantly sharing bad news. It wasn't exactly what Anne wanted to hear, but she appreciated that Mildred would share the rumors with her. Most people would not, and Anne would prefer to know rather than not know.

"They make a big deal out of the fact that Wendy is no longer on the steering committee," Mildred continued.

Anne shook her head. "That's just temporary. She voluntarily excused herself until the police have cleared her." Of course, Wendy had actually been asked to excuse herself, but Anne clung to the fact that she had taken the step willingly. "And wasn't there a quote in the paper from the police saying that they had no viable suspects?"

Mildred shrugged. "I'm afraid that until the police clear the matter up, people will feel the need to suspect *someone*. For the moment, many seem to find Wendy a convenient suspect." She paused. "But of course, not everyone does. Some of the stories going around are so wild you forget entirely about poor Wendy. Complicated heists like you'd see in the movies."

"Seriously?" Anne asked.

"It's the second vase, I think," Mildred said in a thoughtful tone. "That detail seems to really capture the imagination. Stealing the first vase seems pretty straightforward, but why leave a second one behind? The story is that it wasn't even a very good match for the stolen one."

Anne nodded. Mildred had said nothing about the value of the second vase, so perhaps that information hadn't gotten out yet.

"Anyway," Mildred continued, "I think people are talking about that far more than they are about Wendy."

Anne appreciated Mildred's efforts to reassure her, and she could readily believe that the second vase was a hot topic. But that didn't mean people weren't talking about Wendy as well.

Wanting to change the subject, Anne said, "Oh, Mildred, I meant to tell you—look what I've found." She picked a volume off her desk and handed it to her.

"Edie's book!" Mildred exclaimed. "How lovely. I remember how proud she was when it was published. She gave me a copy with a lovely inscription." She opened the book and began to page through it. "I'm afraid I haven't looked at it in ages, but I remember how much she enjoyed working on it. I would get daily updates on its progress. And she did such a fine job too!" Mildred closed the book and patted its cover. "Do you still have her collection of dolls?"

"Yes. I've decided to have them appraised at the Railroad Days event."

Mildred nodded approvingly. "I don't know if they're worth anything, but I know that your aunt Edie considered them to be especially fine examples." She gestured with the book. "And she had the knowledge to make such a judgment. I'll be very interested to hear what you learn about them."

"Well, I don't know their value, either," Anne said, "but I asked Wendy to do a little research, and she seems to think that they may actually be worth something."

"So much the better," said Mildred with a nod, and then she paused. A flicker of worry danced over her face. "Are you thinking of putting them in the auction?"

"Oh no," Anne replied with a laugh. "Not those. No, I still need to find something to donate to the auction."

At that point Remi called for Anne to answer a patron's question, and Anne had to excuse herself from her conversation with Mildred. With Bella and Remi handling the ordinary duties, Anne was kept busy circulating throughout the building to help people find books, conduct research, use the computers, and get the most out of the library's services. She made sure to check periodically on Ben and Liddie, who spent the morning reading in a corner of the Children's Room.

Anne was constantly up and down the stairs, going from the Children's Room to the Fiction Room to the History Room as she responded to questions. Since she passed through the Children's Room so regularly, it was easy to glance at her children or stop to say a quick word as she went by.

She was also pleased to see the number of people, both children and adults, who were examining the display she had created around the Martin Luther King Jr. biography and civil rights histories. At one point, she was surprised to see even Gertrude Haines turning away from the display and making her way back to the stairs. Anne hadn't seen her enter the library, and she briefly considered trying to catch up to her to say hello and make her feel welcome. But she was already in the middle of another errand.

Still, it appeared that writing a column for the newspaper was an excellent way to bring new people into the library. She'd certainly never seen Gertrude there before. And since it was Anne's job to make sure that the community was aware of all the library had to offer, she was more pleased that she had agreed to Grace's suggestion. Briefly she wondered whether she ought to move the entire display downstairs in order to make it more accessible.

But no, she decided, the books and the display had been created specifically for the Children's Room. It was doing the most good right where it was.

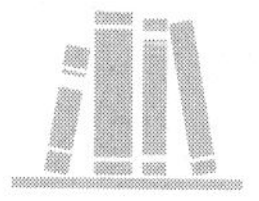

Chapter Eleven

Anne felt that she was able to catch her breath again on Tuesday. The number of visitors was back to its usual weekday level, and Wendy had come in for her volunteer shift. Still, the activity of the weekend reminded Anne that summer was here, and that would mean a larger number of children in the library on a regular basis. She'd better review her staffing and schedules to make sure that she was prepared.

Wendy was still subdued, and Anne could tell that she was trying hard not to show the depth of her distress. She had taken to making jokes about herself as "the master criminal" and trying to decide what her next crime should be.

"What should my name be?" she suddenly asked.

Anne cocked an eyebrow and asked, "What's wrong with *Wendy*?"

"No, no. My criminal mastermind name. My special alias. You know, like Cary Grant was the Cat in *To Catch a Thief*."

"Cary Grant turned out not to be the thief in that movie. He was wrongly suspected." Anne emphasized the last words, but Wendy ignored her.

"What's another cool animal? The Fox? They're clever and sneaky. The Owl? Wise but perhaps not very criminal. The Jackal? No, that one's been used as well. Come on, Anne, help me out."

Anne looked at her friend, unsure whether it was better to humor her or ignore her. Finally she said, "How about the Stoat?"

"The Stoat," Wendy repeated reflectively. "That's a big weasel, right? You could be on to something there."

"And then, when you had your winter coat, you would be the Ermine," Anne continued. "Ermine is associated with royalty."

"*Bah!* What does a criminal mastermind have to do with royalty?"

"Well, if you want a name that fits your character, you'd have to be the Mom," Anne suggested.

"Also not a name for a criminal mastermind," Wendy replied, though this did produce a small but genuine smile. "Though my kids might disagree..."

Her brief smile notwithstanding, however, Wendy was clearly still upset, and Anne once again felt an overwhelming urge to find some way to help. She announced that she had to run an errand and slipped upstairs to her apartment, leaving the library in Wendy's hands.

Anne flipped through the phone book to find the number for the Blue Hill Railroad Museum. Since she wasn't sure of the hours the museum was open, she was pleased when she was able to get Hal McCollum on the line. She asked if he would have a few minutes to talk with her if she were to come down right away.

He was pacing in the museum's main hall when she arrived. The museum building had originally been a railroad station, and the doors opened directly into the main hall of what had once been the station's spacious waiting room. As soon as Hal spotted her, he immediately came forward.

"Anne," he said, wringing his hands, "allow me to say again how sorry I am that this has happened. I feel just terrible that this occurred here at the museum. I hope that the police will be able to recover your vase."

Anne inwardly cringed at his use of *your*, but considering what she wanted from Hal, she didn't contradict him. Instead, she said, "Thank you. I was hoping that you might be able to help me understand better just *how* it happened." She watched his body stiffen, as if he had absorbed a blow. "You know, explain your security systems and whatnot. If you don't mind, that is."

He hesitated for just a fraction of a second before saying, "No, of course not. I'd be happy to show you the security arrangements." But he stood rooted to the spot. The wringing of his hands intensified. "It's just...I wondered...Anne, are you thinking of bringing some kind of action against the museum? Because if that's the case, then maybe I shouldn't show you anything. At least, not without my lawyer."

"Action?" Anne asked, startled. "No, I..."

"Because you did sign that consent form, Anne. You remember? I took it over to the library and you signed it."

Anne realized that Hal was worried about the museum's potential liability for the theft. Since the idea of suing the museum had never occurred to her, she hadn't anticipated this response. But when she thought about the stress she had felt at the suggestion that the library might face some sort of liability, she could sympathize completely with his concern.

"No, Hal," she said firmly. "I'm not thinking about any sort of action against the museum. Not at all. " She watched while her words and her tone registered and he relaxed.

His face broke out in a grin. "Well, I must say that comes as a relief." He heaved a sigh and then tried to suppress his smile. "I mean, I really do feel terrible about what happened, you know."

"I know you do," Anne said, smiling herself. "And I'm sorry that it happened too. But to tell you truth, there's something that I'm more upset about."

Hal raised an eyebrow in question.

"It's about Wendy," Anne explained.

Hal nodded. "Shall we go back to the office?" He turned and gestured toward the museum's back rooms.

"It's been very upsetting for her," Anne said once they were settled at a small round table in Hal's office. "The idea that she might be a suspect..."

"But surely the police don't really suspect her, do they?" Hal exclaimed. "That would be ridiculous."

"No, I don't think they really do," Anne allowed, "but there's still this whole business of who's been cleared and who has not. And of course, the committee..." She gestured vaguely. She didn't want to sound accusing since Hal was himself a member of the committee.

Hal looked down with a troubled expression. "I know, I know. "It was a very difficult discussion for everyone." He brought his head back up. "But it was her own choice in the end, you know. She understood the concerns as well as anybody, better even. And it's only temporary."

Anne nodded to show that she was aware of all this.

"But yes," Hal went on, "I can see that it would still be upsetting."

"And all that does nothing to stop the rumors," Anne pointed out. "I want to do something to help her, and the only thing I can think of is to try to understand how all this happened. Who knows, maybe I'll be able to think of something that will clear Wendy completely."

Hal gave her an odd look. "The police..."

"Oh, I'm not conducting an investigation," Anne reassured him. "I'm just trying to come to a better understanding. Because I'm a librarian, and that's what I do—I research things. Maybe in the process of research, I'll find something or think of something that will help Wendy."

Hal looked thoughtful for a few moments, and then spread his hands. "How can I help?"

* * *

"We have no alarm system," Hal explained as they toured the facility. "We can't afford it. And to tell you the truth, it just wouldn't be justified. We do have good doors and good, solid locks, though." He gestured at the main display room. "Most of our collection is historically significant, but it doesn't really have great financial value. We have a few nice artifacts that a serious collector of railroad memorabilia would like to have, but really, the chances of anyone going to the trouble of stealing something like that are pretty slim."

"But I thought there was extra security now because of all the donations for the auction," Anne said.

Hal nodded. "That's right," but the extra security is in the form of people, not technology." He led her across the floor to the large display case that had held the vase. It now contained a well-worn boxed clock and a typed index card that read *Hamilton WWII-era deck watch chronometer.*

"We put many items from our regular collection in storage in order to make space to display the auction items," he said. "We selected this case to hold the vase in order to show it off a bit." He touched the bottom edge of one side of the case. "This side swings open like this."

The case popped open at Hal's touch.

"Doesn't it lock?" Anne asked, surprised.

Hal shook his head. "Sadly, almost all of our display cases are thirdhand, or even fourth. Usually, someone was getting rid of them *because* the locks no longer worked, or they'd lost the key, or whatever. When we were setting up the museum, we just didn't have the money to invest in better cases. And again, it's not like the need was pressing."

"Still," said Anne, "it would be pretty easy for someone to get in there, get the vase out, leave the other one, and then close the door with no one being the wiser."

She looked around the room. The display cabinet was off to one side, close to a wall rather than in the middle of the room, but it was taller than the other cases, most of which only came up to her waist.

Curious, Anne made a circuit of the room, looking at the cabinet from various angles. The cabinet's position didn't command attention, but it was plainly visible from almost any place in the room, for anyone who happened to be looking. The thief must have acted quickly to get the case open and switch the vases without calling attention to himself. Unless the theft had occurred when the museum was closed.

Hal also gave Anne a tour of the storerooms and offices in the back. Two doors gave access to the back of the museum, plus a large garage-type door that provided access for larger items. But as Hal pointed out, these doors were all even heavier and more solid than the front door. "And we check these every night as part of the lockup procedure," he said. All the lower windows on the back of the building were protected by bars or grates.

As Hal led Anne through a long workroom, she noticed that it was divided up into stations. "I hadn't realized how much goes on back here," she exclaimed.

"Those are the work spaces we've set up for the experts Miles Bridges has been bringing in. There's quite a crowd of them, and each one needs space to do his or her thing. Of course, they only come in once in a while to look at whatever new donations have been made for the auction, but they all want to have some space of their own to use when they're here. If I'd realized just how much space it was going to take, I wouldn't have agreed to it. But it's too late now, and they come and go at all hours."

Anne looked at him sharply. "At all hours? Do they all have keys?"

Hal sighed. "Yes, and it's not just them. Most of the extra security people have keys, and there were already many longtime volunteers for the museum who had keys, as well as the museum's board of directors. *And* the members of the steering committee had keys." He shrugged. "Unfortunately, there are a lot of keys out there. The police gave me a pretty hard time about that. But what are we going to do? When you have an organization that depends so heavily on volunteers, you have to give them access. This whole auction business just made things worse."

"But the bottom line is that there are a lot of people who could have slipped in when the museum was closed and taken the vase," Anne said thoughtfully.

"That's the view of the police," Hal said, "and I could see why they would think that. But these people are all trustworthy. It makes no more sense to accuse them than to think Wendy did it. After all, Wendy had a key herself."

As they walked back to the front of the building, Anne felt very frustrated. Stealing the vase would have been very straightforward. Many people had access to the museum even when it was closed, and pretty much anyone had access to the display cabinet, provided they had a few moments of privacy.

But though almost anyone could have stolen the vase, she'd learned nothing that shed any light on why. The answer seemed obvious—the vase was worth a lot of money, and due to the news article about it, that fact was public knowledge. But that didn't explain why someone would go to the trouble of replacing it with a second vase, and especially not one that might be just as valuable as the stolen one.

And so what if the vase was valuable? Just because you knew something was worth a lot of money didn't mean that it was easy to turn it into cash.

She realized that she'd been staring at the display cabinet for some time while Hal McCollum waited expectantly. She turned to him and smiled. "I'm sorry, Hal. Thank you so much for all your help."

"Are you going back to the library?" he asked.

Anne nodded.

"Perhaps I'll walk up with you, if I may. I read your column in the paper. I enjoyed it very much, and I'd like to see the book display you described."

Soon they stood before the display in the Children's Room, and Hal looked at the pictures with great interest. "Some of them are quite startling," he observed, "but I'm so glad to see that you've done this. It's too easy to forget the ugly and unpleasant aspects of history, but we do a disservice to ourselves and our children—and to the people who lived through it—when we don't remember."

Anne agreed wholeheartedly, but she couldn't help thinking of the disservice this theft and the rumors surrounding it were doing to Wendy.

Chapter Twelve

Anne began the next morning at her desk with a cup of coffee and the new edition of the *Blue Hill Gazette*. Of course, this week's *Gazette* didn't have the same excitement for her as last week's, when her first book column had run, but at least the story about the stolen vase had moved off the front page due to the lack of police progress.

Anne enjoyed her thorough read of the paper until she came to the opinion page at the end. This was where the *Gazette* ran letters to the editor, and to her surprise, there were two letters in response to her column. The first had been written by Mildred Farley and was full of praise for Anne's efforts. But Anne's heart sank as she read the second.

The second letter had been written by an indignant Gertrude Haines. Though she didn't come out and say it in so many words, Gertrude strongly hinted that Martin Luther King Jr. was a poor role model for children, though she gave no reasons for this. Gertrude was particularly critical of the images from the civil rights era that Anne had mounted as part of the display in the Children's Room at the library. She declared these images much too violent and disturbing to be included in a display for children and implied that Anne, in creating the display, had been driven by an ideological agenda rather than a sincere concern for the children who visited her library.

Her library.

Shocked and saddened, Anne sat back and considered the letter. She had received so much positive feedback on both the column and the display that she was thunderstruck to read such a critical response. More than that, she immediately began to question her own motives to determine if Gertrude's accusations were in any way true.

The piece of the letter that bothered her the most was the phrase "her library." As if Anne would use the library as some sort of soapbox for airing her own personal opinions. This was an insult not only to Anne personally but to her professionalism as a librarian. Moreover, it was an insult to the memory of Aunt Edie, who had left her home to the town so that *all* the residents of Blue Hill might have a library—including Gertrude Haines. The library belonged to Blue Hill, not to Anne.

So what should she do? Anne tried to set her emotions aside and consider the matter objectively.

Her primary responsibility was to nurture a library that would serve as many citizens as possible, as skillfully as possible. It bothered her to know that one of her patrons was upset enough to publicly criticize the library, since that might turn away other people who could benefit from the library's services.

On the other hand, it was impossible to please everyone all the time, and those who were displeased had a right to express their opinions. The real question was whether this response was an anomaly or if it was shared by more people in the community.

The other question was how, or even whether, she should respond. Should she write a letter in response, defending her display? Or should she alter the display in order to appease Gertrude and any others who might be upset?

Anne decided to do nothing for the time being. She would try to figure out if this was a general concern among the public or the opinion of a single individual.

Though she'd made her decision, Anne couldn't help worrying about Gertrude's letter as the morning wore on. After some debate, she decided to clip the letter from the paper to preserve it in a file. She needed to keep a record of the bad along with the good if the library was to grow and improve over time.

Later that morning, Grace Hawkins walked in. She gave Anne a tentative smile. "So have you seen today's edition?"

As soon as Grace came through the door, Anne had steeled herself to be nonchalant. She didn't want Grace to think Anne was too sensitive or to regret her decision to have Anne write a column. "Oh yes," she replied, trying to sound cheerful, "it looks like the score so far is one to one." She'd been so focused on the critical letter that it was only at the last moment that she recalled Mildred's letter of praise.

Grace didn't seem fooled by Anne's cheerful demeanor. "It's not about keeping score," she said solemnly. "I just wanted to be sure you were okay. The first time you get a letter like that, it can be a little disconcerting. Believe me, I know." When Anne said nothing, Grace continued, "Well, I did tell you there would be feedback."

Anne nodded. Grace had warned her. Anne just hadn't realized what she'd meant.

Grace hesitated. "You understand why I ran the letter, though, right? Our policy has to be pretty broad. We're a platform for public opinion. So unless a letter is obviously false or libelous, we're going to run it, even if it's critical or controversial."

"Oh, of course," Anne said quickly. "I understand completely. I wouldn't expect you to suppress a letter just because it was critical. People have a right to express their opinions." Anne believed this wholeheartedly, no matter how much this particular opinion bothered her.

Grace relaxed. "Good. And as you say, you're one for one, which is actually quite good, since most people don't bother to write unless they're upset about something. Believe me, letters of praise are far more rare than letters of criticism. So no matter what it feels like, you're actually ahead of the game."

Anne gave a rueful smile. "I thought you weren't keeping score," she said, but she was reassured by Grace's words and grateful to Mildred for making the effort to write. It was just the kind of support that Aunt Edie would have provided. Better in a way, since Mildred wasn't a relative.

"You know," Grace said slowly, "you have as much right to send in a letter as anyone."

Anne shook her head. "I thought about it, but I don't see the point. I doubt I could change her mind. Besides, I don't think I should get into a public debate with everyone who disagrees with me. Everyone is entitled to their own opinion, and there's no law that says we all have to agree." She paused. "If it turns out that there are many people who feel the way she does, then I might reconsider, but for the moment, I think that publicly disagreeing with a single critic just makes me look intolerant, which is not the image that I want the library to project."

Grace smiled at her, a broad, genuine smile. "I think that's best. After all, everyone who's mentioned the column to me had nothing but good things to say. I think it's going to be a hit."

"I hope so!" Anne laughed. "Now that I've written one, I can't wait to write more."

Grace winked at her. "I knew you'd get hooked."

* * *

"She's nothing but a busybody," Wendy said vehemently. She had also stopped by the library to reassure Anne after reading Gertrude Haines's letter in the paper.

Though Anne appreciated the support, she was even more pleased that this incident had taken Wendy's mind off her troubles over the stolen vase.

"I can't say I know her that well," Anne replied mildly.

"I was on a committee with her at church one time," Wendy said. "Everything had to be done exactly her way. Even when everyone had decided on something else, even when we had *voted* on it, she kept coming back and making the same arguments again. We'd say, 'We already decided that,' but it didn't stop her. She just kept harping on it. Sometimes we'd change the decision just to get some peace, but there were a few times where she never got her way, and once the committee's work was done, all she did was critique the rest of us." She shook her head. "Nobody asks her to serve on committees anymore."

"She sounds like a piece of work," said Anne, who secretly found Wendy's description rather gratifying.

"And I don't know where she gets off commenting on what's age appropriate for children," Wendy continued. "She doesn't have any of her own."

"Well," said Anne, "it's not an absolute requirement. I've known a number of childless people who still understood children very well."

"And plenty of people who *do* have children are still terrible parents. I know. But it's just so typical of her behavior."

Anne was saved from trying to respond to this by the entrance of Reverend Tom and Maggie Sloan.

"Anne," Maggie called out, "that was such a lovely letter from Mildred in the paper today. I thought her comments were spot on."

"Hers wasn't the only letter," Wendy muttered.

Reverend Tom turned to her with a twinkle in his eye. "I feel like we've walked into the middle of a conversation."

"Come on, Reverend," Wendy said, "you know what she's like."

"I admit she's sometimes a troubled member of the flock," Reverend Tom said. "But then again, so are we all, at times."

He arched an eyebrow at Wendy, who clearly took his point. He turned to Anne. "But I trust you're taking it in stride, Anne?"

Anne glanced at Wendy, then looked down. "Well, I admit I was a little taken aback when I first read it."

Reverend Tom nodded. "Naturally."

"But then, I figured there will always be people who disagree with me. If I'm going to put myself out there by writing a column for the newspaper, then I need to be prepared for people to express their opinions."

He nodded. "I knew you would keep a healthy perspective on it."

The four of them continued to chat, and Anne noticed that Reverend Tom and Maggie carefully avoided mentioning Railroad Days, the auction, or the stolen vase. Anne had been working hard to avoid these topics with Wendy herself, so she knew just how difficult it was to steer clear of subjects that were on the lips of the entire town.

Once the Sloans and Wendy were gone, Anne began to second-guess herself about Gertrude Haines's letter. Was she taking the matter too lightly? After all, Grace, Wendy, Reverend Tom, and Maggie had *all* come by to console her. Perhaps their actions were speaking louder than their words? Perhaps the advice not to let it bother her was offered precisely because it *ought* to be bothering her?

The library door opened and Alex Ochs entered. *Oh no*, Anne thought, *here we go again*.

Her suspicions were confirmed when he offered an extra-cheerful, "Hi, Anne! I just stopped by to see how you're doing."

"Yes, I saw it," she said, deciding to stop this conversation before it started. "And yes, it bothered me a little at first, but I'm trying to take it in stride, and yes, I appreciate your interest, and everybody's interest, and I know you all mean well, but I'm tired of talking about it at the moment."

"Um, okay," said Alex, looking confused.

Anne still couldn't let it go entirely. "I mean, it's just one letter to the editor, right? Even if everyone in town *does* read the *Gazette*." She sighed and looked at him. "Okay, tell me, what did you think when you read it?"

"Oh," said Alex brightly, "I haven't had a chance to read the paper yet."

Chapter Thirteen

The next day, Anne was surprised to get a phone call from Miles Bridges.

"Anne," he said, "when you were here last week, you asked if I would deliver a message to the vase's donor. Well, I talked with him, and he agreed to reveal his identity."

"I see," Anne said, rather surprised. She juggled a stack of returned books.

"In fact," Miles continued, "today is the day that we have arranged for him to talk with the police. And he suggested that if you wanted to go down to the police station this afternoon, you could meet him then."

"I see," Anne said again, still more surprised. "Well, yes, of course. I would like that very much."

He gave her the time and hung up.

Anne spent the next twenty minutes calling her volunteers until Betty Bultman agreed to come in on short notice.

* * *

When she arrived at the station, Anne told the receptionist that she was meeting Miles Bridges, and she was immediately led to a conference room in the back, where three other people had already assembled. Aside from Miles, who paced by the windows, an extremely elderly man sat at one end of the conference table, while a middle-aged man sat near him.

As soon as Anne was shown in, Miles came forward. "Thank you for coming on such short notice, Anne. Mr. Stratton decided that since he'd agreed to meet all of you, he'd better do so all at once."

As Miles spoke, the elderly man looked up at Anne, while the younger man glanced back and forth between them. Slowly, the elderly man got to his feet, assisted both by the younger man and by his cane, and Miles waited respectfully until he was standing.

Then he said in a louder voice, "Anne Gibson, this is Percy Stratton and his nephew, Ronald Hollis."

Though standing, Mr. Stratton did not move, and Anne stepped forward to shake first his hand and then Mr. Hollis's.

Percy Stratton was frail and palsied, with sunken eyes blurred behind thick glasses. He wore an old-fashioned tweed suit that hung loosely on him, as if he had lost weight in his old age. The grip of his handshake was practically nonexistent.

The nephew was somewhat ill at ease, though he was clearly considerate of his uncle. Unlike his uncle though, Mr. Hollis was tall and ruddy cheeked. He wore a sport coat and dress shirt and tie over jeans and brown oxford shoes. Anne guessed he was a professor.

"Mr. Stratton," Anne said, speaking loudly and distinctly as Miles had done, "it's quite a pleasure." Percy Stratton nodded and offered a smile but said nothing. "The first thing I should do," Anne continued, "is thank you for the very generous donation that you intended to give to the library. Despite the... unfortunate developments, we are still very grateful. Thank you."

Mr. Stratton replied in a high-pitched, quavery voice, "You're very welcome. Didn't intend for things to go the way they did, of course, but the best-laid plans, eh?" He gestured toward the chairs around the table, and with his nephew's help, lowered himself back down into his own. "Best-laid plans," he muttered again with a sigh.

Anne glanced at Miles and at Ronald Hollis, but neither seemed inclined to pick up the conversation, so she leaned forward and said, "I couldn't help but be curious, Mr. Stratton, why you chose the library for your philanthropy." She paused but couldn't tell whether he was taking in the question. "It comes as quite a surprise," she continued, "since you and I hadn't met until now."

Percy Stratton offered a weak smile, but he gave no sign that he understood her. After a moment, he turned to his nephew, and Mr. Hollis spoke in an even louder voice. "She's asking why you gave the vase to the library, Uncle Percy," he explained.

The old man turned back in Anne's direction. "To help out, of course. The vase is worth some money, or so they tell me. So I thought, auction it off, give the money to the library. The library could always use some more money, eh?" Mr. Stratton nodded at her encouragingly.

"Yes, sir," Anne said, "that's certainly true."

The old man cackled as if the appeal of more money was a private joke between them. Then he continued, "It was a right smart thing that Ms. Edie did, setting up that library. Right smart lady." His attention seemed to drift for a moment, then refocused on Anne. "Ms. Edie Summers. Do you know her?"

Anne nodded. "She was my great-aunt." Then, to give him time to process this, she added, "My father's aunt."

Mr. Stratton nodded. "Certainly, certainly. Right smart."

Anne hesitated. He hadn't really answered the question about why he'd chosen the library, but she couldn't figure out how to ask it again. Instead, she said, "How did you know my aunt?" And when he looked a little vague, she said, "How did you know Edie Summers?"

"Oh, I didn't," Mr. Stratton replied. "'At least not really, no." His attention seemed to wander off again.

Puzzled, Anne looked to Ronald Hollis, but he just shrugged. She was about to ask him a question about himself when Michael Banks came into the room.

When he saw that there were four people there, he looked at them in dismay. "Miles," he said, turning to the antiques dealer, "I wanted to interview Mr. Stratton."

"Well, yes," Miles began meekly, "but as I explained, his nephew, well, he needs his nephew to... help him out."

"And, Anne," Michael asked, turning to her, "what are you doing here?"

"Well, Anne wanted to meet Mr. Stratton as well," Miles explained, "and Mr. Stratton suggested that as long as he was coming down here anyway, then she might as well come too."

Michael looked at them all for a moment, considering. "I'm going to ask Anne and Miles to wait out in the waiting room. Mr. Hollis, is it? I'd prefer to interview your uncle alone, but..."

Mr. Hollis looked up. "I feel strongly that I should stay with him. "Given his age, and all."

Michael looked closely at Percy Stratton, who scowled and didn't really seem to follow the conversation. He sighed. "Okay, then, you'll stay here. But just the two of you."

Anne got up to join Miles by the door. "But we can wait?" she asked.

Michael's face assumed a resigned expression. "Yes," he said. "You may wait."

* * *

What Michael called the waiting room was really just a couple of chairs in a corner of the lobby, opposite the receptionist's desk. The two chairs had seen hard use and were too low to be comfortable. A tall, spindly plant stood between the chairs, and Anne sat so low that its long, spear-like leaves brushed the top of her head.

There was considerable traffic back and forth through the lobby, and though most of those passing through waved or spoke to the receptionist, there seemed to be little call for her to actually receive anyone. But she had kindly offered beverages to Anne, who declined, and Miles, who accepted a glass of water. When he finished it, Anne noticed, he had no place to set the plastic cup. He looked about forlornly for a moment and then rested it on his knee.

"He seems like a nice man," Anne tried, and when Miles looked her way, she added, "Mr. Stratton."

"Yes," he replied quickly. "Very nice. Though prickly at times." He chuckled and added, "Most of the time."

"Have you known him and his nephew long?"

"I've known Percy for many years. He lives on the outskirts of State College in a house absolutely crammed with stuff. Much of it's junk, of course, but he also has some very nice antiques. I've been able to help him out a few times over the years when he wanted to sell something." He paused and frowned. "The nephew I've only known for a year or so. He lives in Pittsburgh, but he seems to be spending more and more time at Percy's, helping him." He sighed sadly. "But then, he needs it, poor old fellow. You're not seeing him as he was in his prime."

"So that's how you came to help him with the donation of the vase? Because you've known him so long?"

"That's right." Miles nodded. "Though this is the first time I've known him to do something like this. He's sold off some of his antiques from time to time, but I've never known him to donate one like this."

"Do *you* know why he chose the library?"

Miles looked at her with confusion in his eyes. "You know, Anne, I really don't. I asked him when he first proposed the idea, but he gave the impression that he really didn't want to talk about it. And it wasn't any of my business." He shrugged. "And of course, I was so pleased to have something of such value in the auction that I didn't want to press the point and risk him changing his mind."

The conversation seemed to be making Miles somewhat melancholy, so Anne tried to change the subject. "And how is work on the auction going?"

"Oh, splendidly," he said, sitting up straighter in his chair with an eager light in his eye. He launched into detailed descriptions of some of his favorite items that had been donated. Most of these ended with a variation on, "Not really valuable, of course, but very interesting," or "but a fine example of its type," or "but in excellent condition." A few of his descriptions ended with, "I wouldn't mind having that in my shop," which seemed to be his highest praise for an item.

But his enthusiasm was infectious, and Anne happily listened to his descriptions of the auction items. "My goodness, Miles," she said at one point, "you know so much about different artifacts and styles."

"Oh well," he replied modestly. "To be successful as a dealer, you have to know a little bit about a lot of things, but of course, I'm not really an expert in any of them. I can often make a good ballpark guess about something's value or origin, but there are only a couple of areas where I can claim any real expertise. That's why I've been lining up so many true experts to help out with the appraisal day and the auction."

"Oh yes, like that Ms. Staub I met."

"*Ye-es*," Miles replied, with a slight hesitation. "Though most of the experts I've brought in are people I've worked with over the years. Ms. Staub, I must confess, is not someone I know very well. She was recommended by a mutual acquaintance. But we're lucky to have her, since Asian ceramics have turned out to be such an important category in the auction. I never would have expected that, but there you are. There's always bound to be some surprises when it comes to antiques." He paused, and then added in a musing tone, "I wonder if he'd allow her to look at the rest of them."

"I'm sorry?" said Anne, puzzled.

"Percy," Miles clarified. "He has a small collection of vases. I was just wondering if he would allow Ms. Staub to examine them."

"Are they all as valuable as the one that was stolen?" After she'd asked, Anne suddenly worried that her question was indiscreet.

If Miles objected, however, he gave no sign. Instead, he shook his head rather sadly. "I couldn't say. I've never had the chance to examine them myself. Percy's funny that way. He makes up his own mind about what he wants to sell, and only then does he let me have a good look. I've been trying to get him to show me his vases for years, but I never saw one up close until he called me about donating that one."

"But you think he'd allow Ms. Staub to do so?"

"Well, no, not really." Miles shook his head. "It just seems like such an opportunity when we have a real expert on hand. But I doubt he'd agree." His face grew thoughtful. "Still, Percy seems to have some knowledge about his collection. When he picks out something to sell, it's almost always something that will fetch a good price. And when he brought me that vase, he said that he'd been told long ago that it was one of the most valuable in his collection. But who told him or when, he wouldn't say."

Anne tried to square this description of an alert and informed antiques owner with the vacant-looking man she had left behind in the conference room. "Perhaps he doesn't remember," she suggested.

Miles gave her a reproachful look, then sighed. "This really isn't one of his good days," he replied after a moment. "It's a shame that this ended up being the day he came in to talk to the police. But Mr. Hollis was insistent that he come along, and this was the first day he could manage it."

Anne thought about the ravages of age. One of Aunt Edie's greatest fears had been losing her mental faculties. Anne was thankful that this hadn't happened, but many people were not so fortunate as her aunt had been.

She was about to question Miles further when Michael Banks emerged from the back, leading a slowly moving Percy Stratton, who was closely followed by his nephew. Michael thanked them again for coming in, but he muttered something about needing to excuse himself and disappeared without further conversation with Miles or Anne.

They had both risen when Mr. Stratton and Mr. Hollis appeared, and they all now stood somewhat awkwardly facing each other.

After a moment, Mr. Hollis said, "Well, it was nice meeting you, Mrs. Gibson," and took his uncle's elbow.

Anne quickly said, "Actually, Mr. Hollis, I was hoping to invite you and your uncle back to the see the library. And you too, of course, Miles," she added, assuming he had driven them. "I don't think Mr. Stratton has actually seen the library." She smiled at him and continued, "I think I'd remember him if he'd been in. Perhaps I could offer you all some tea."

Mr. Stratton had begun nodding while she was still talking, and he said, "Thank you, thank you," in a vague but expectant tone.

But his nephew quickly cut in. "That's very kind of you, but I'm afraid I have to get my uncle home and then be on my way."

"I'm sorry to hear it." Anne turned more fully to Mr. Stratton. "Miles tells me that you live in State College, Mr. Stratton. Perhaps you'd allow me to come by and visit you sometime? Since you seem to take an interest in our library?"

Mr. Hollis frowned and began, "I don't..."

But this time it was Mr. Stratton who cut in. "Of course, young lady. I'd be delighted." Moreover, he seemed to be having a sudden moment of greater lucidity, or at least it seemed so to Anne. "What would you say to coming by on Monday?"

Anne, somewhat taken aback, said, "Thank you Mr. Stratton. I'd like that very much." After a moment, she added, "I'm sure I can get directions to your house from Miles." She glanced at him inquiringly, and after a brief hesitation, he nodded.

"Until then," said Percy Stratton, reaching out with his feeble grip once again. "Remarkable lady, your aunt." And he started for the door, trailed by Mr. Hollis and Miles. "Remarkable lady."

Chapter Fourteen

So you have no idea what they talked about?" The frustration in Wendy's voice was evident. She had passed through trying to laugh off the situation and had settled into simple and unrelieved distress.

Anne had promised to share every scrap of news that she received about the investigation, and so the next day she told Wendy about meeting Percy Stratton and Ronald Hollis. At any other time, Anne knew, Wendy would have been fascinated to learn the identity of the mysterious benefactor, but now the only relevant point was that the meeting didn't seem to have advanced the investigation.

"No, Michael kicked us out of the conference room. But I'm going to visit Mr. Stratton myself on Monday."

"I know," Wendy replied. "And I appreciate it, I really do. But what will you be able to find by yourself?'" She sighed. "I'm sorry, I don't mean to sound ungrateful. But you see what I mean?"

"Of course, I do. And you're right, I'm probably not going to be able to help. But at least I can try."

Wendy gave her a weak smile of gratitude.

Anne added, "I've got to apply my research skills to something, eh?"

Wendy sighed, not even acknowledging Anne's attempt at humor. "I can't imagine he was able to tell the police anything useful anyway. After all, it was stolen after it left his possession. What could he know about it?"

Anne shrugged. "I don't know. Perhaps he was approached in the past by somebody who wanted to buy it and he refused to sell." Even as she said these words, something about the idea tugged at the back of Anne's mind.

Wendy asked, "How would that help?"

Anne, her attention divided by the nagging but untraceable thought, said, "It would at least give them the name of someone who definitely wanted to own that vase himself."

"Anne, it's a ten-thousand-dollar vase!" Wendy exclaimed, breaking Anne's concentration. "There's no shortage of people who would want it."

This reminded Anne of another train of thought. "A vase that's worth ten thousand dollars," she said thoughtfully, "is not the same thing as having ten thousand dollars."

"What do you mean?"

"It comes down to the question of the thief's motives. Does he want the vase for itself, or does he want the money it's worth?"

Wendy's own face grew thoughtful, and she nodded.

"If it's the former," Anne continued, "then he's probably a collector or expert, someone who's a member of a fairly small community."

"He's also pretty wealthy," Wendy observed, and when Anne gave her a questioning look, she continued, "It's a ten-thousand-dollar vase! Anyone who wants it and *doesn't* want the money out of it must have plenty himself already."

Anne nodded. "Okay, but given the kind of person we're describing—knowledgeable, wealthy, presumably someone with status—how likely is it that he'd steal the vase himself?"

"You mean he would have hired a professional?" Wendy asked. "Is that what the police think?"

Anne shook her head. "They haven't said anything of the sort." But she made a mental note to discuss the possibility with Michael Banks.

Wendy looked dissatisfied. "I see your point, but I'm not sure we can count on that idea. Greed makes people do strange things, even people who already have plenty. And hiring a third party makes the wealthy collector, who is presumably someone of prominence, vulnerable to the thief."

"Committing the crime himself makes him vulnerable to getting caught," Anne countered, "but I see what you're saying."

She thought for a moment. "So what about our other hypothetical thief? The one who wants the vase for its value? Presumably he wants to turn it into cash as soon as possible. How does he do that?"

"He'd have to find a dealer," Wendy said quickly.

Anne nodded. "And the police *are* checking with dealers," she said. "He'd have to find one that's either crooked or who doesn't recognize the vase as stolen."

"At this point, who could *that* be? Hey, don't thieves have special connections for stolen goods?" Wendy asked. "What do they call them? Fences?"

Anne sighed. "That sort of thing is way beyond our knowledge," though I do wonder if a fence would be able to handle something as specialized as an antique Chinese vase."

"Perhaps they specialize the way legitimate dealers do?" Wendy suggested.

"But even if they do, does our thief know how to find someone like that? But on the other hand, if he just goes to a 'regular' fence, can he get anything close to the vase's worth?"

"So I guess it depends on our thief's knowledge and connections," Wendy suggested.

Anne nodded. "Did he steal the vase because he already knew how to get rid of it and turn it into cash? Or did he just read in the paper about how valuable it was and couldn't resist the temptation?"

They both pondered the question in silence for a few moments, and then Wendy sat back and let out a long sigh. For a while, as they had discussed the possibilities, Wendy's face had shown some of her old energy, but now she looked even more dejected than before.

"That's the most likely thing, isn't it?" Wendy said. "There was so much media attention to the value of the vase that somebody saw that and just couldn't resist. And now they'll carry it off to New York or someplace and get rid of it in whatever way they can, even if they only get a fraction of its value." She bit her lower lip. "The police will never be able to solve this."

Anne shook her head emphatically. "It can't be as simple as you're describing," she said with confidence. "You're forgetting about the second vase."

Anne studied Wendy's face. Clearly Wendy had, indeed, forgotten about the second vase.

Puzzling out the mystery of the theft and the motives of the thief was interesting, but Anne's primary concern was finding some way to ease her friend's distress. And so far, the best way of doing that seemed to be finding ways to nurture her hopes that the police would solve the crime and lift the cloud of suspicion hanging over her.

"This crime could not have been purely impulsive," Anne said. "The thief planned far enough ahead to secure that second vase and then went to the trouble of leaving it behind to replace the first one. The question is, why?"

Anne was happy to see her friend's expression clear again as she began to wrestle with the question. "I guess I assumed the thief was trying to delay discovery of the crime," Wendy said.

"That's what I thought too," Anne said quickly. "But it didn't work very well, did it? And anyway, doesn't it seem like an awful lot of trouble to go to? Does the thief just happen to have a bunch of Chinese vases lying around, that he can pick one up and bring it with him to make the switch? That seems pretty unlikely. So that means he had to go out and find one someplace. Then he had to sneak it into the museum in order to make the switch and sneak out with the other one. And why even bother? If he already has one valuable vase, why exchange it for another?"

Anne stopped abruptly. Though she had been keeping Wendy informed about the police investigation, she had not mentioned Miles Bridges's suspicions about the value of the second vase. For one thing, Miles was not certain of his on-the-fly evaluation. And for another, Anne wasn't sure the information had been shared with the police yet, and she had felt a need to be discreet.

But Wendy, of course, immediately picked up on her words. "What do you mean, 'already has one valuable vase?' Are you saying that the second vase is valuable too?"

Reluctantly, Anne shared what Miles had told her, emphasizing the fact that he had not thoroughly examined the vase, and therefore, it was information they needed to keep to themselves.

"Whew," said Wendy. "So he steals one vase but replaces it with another that's equally valuable? I'm having a hard time getting my head around that."

"Yes, me too." Anne nodded.

"By the way," Wendy continued, "have you noticed that we keep saying 'he' as though we know it's a man?"

Anne *had* noticed, but in her case it had nothing to do with an assumption about the thief's gender. She had been deliberately saying "he" to reinforce the idea that she did not believe that Wendy could be the thief. Rather than explain this, however, Anne changed the subject.

"You know, instead of focusing on the actual thief, perhaps we should be thinking more about how to poke holes in the theory that you could have done this," Anne suggested. "While I hope the police catch the thief, I'm more concerned about ruling you out."

"Don't you think I've been over that?" Wendy asked plaintively.

"I'm sure you've been over it many times in your own head," Anne said.

"In my head, with my husband, with the police..."

"Well, even still," Anne persisted, "try going over it with me." She hoped that getting Wendy to focus on the details of what happened, rather than speculating about the future, might have a calming effect. "What can you tell me about that night? Isn't there anything that would make it impossible to suspect you?"

Wendy's voice adopted a resigned tone. "It was Saturday night." She spoke as if reciting a lesson learned by rote. "We'd had a committee meeting to go over things that had been donated for the auction. We met in the back room of the museum. We finished up and we all left. As soon as I got home, I realized that I had left my cell phone at the museum."

Wendy's voice warmed up and she began to speak in a more natural tone. "I didn't even turn off the car, because I knew if I didn't go back right then, I wouldn't feel like doing it later. So I turned around in my own driveway and went straight back to the museum."

Wendy's expression grew more focused, and Anne felt that she was sincerely trying now to recall the details of the evening. "I let myself in. Did I mention that all the committee members have keys?" She looked at Anne, who nodded to confirm that she knew this. "It was both neat and spooky," Wendy continued with a bit of the awe that she must have felt at the time. "Not completely dark, because Hal had set up some night-lights as part of the security. But dim and very quiet."

Wendy shook her head. "The cabinets and display cases all seemed larger than they do during the day. Looming. And, I don't know, maybe it's because there are so many old things there, but it just felt solemn and mysterious and... historical." She gave a little laugh at her own description. "And I just stood there for a while, near the entrance, breathing it all in." For a moment, her eyes refocused and she looked at Anne. "After all, how many times do you get to be in a museum when there's nobody else there?"

Anne did not reply, reluctant to disturb the flow of Wendy's memories.

"But of course, that wasn't the case. After I'd stood there for a while, I started to go to the back to the storeroom where we'd been meeting, but I'd only taken a few steps, when suddenly the door to the back rooms opened and somebody came out!" Anne stirred, but she still refrained from speaking. "I was so startled, well, I yelped."

Wendy chuckled at the memory now. "But if I was scared, I wasn't the only one. This voice calls out 'Who's there?' and I could tell from the tone that he was as surprised as I was. Fortunately, I'd recognized him by now as one of the security guards that Hal had brought in, so I just said 'It's me, Wendy Pyle.' And he knew who I was right away."

Anne could no longer contain herself. "I'd forgotten about the security guard. Surely he can tell the police why you were there. You've got to let them know right away!"

Wendy gave her an odd look. "I've done that, Anne, of course I have. But it doesn't prove anything."

"Well, what happened next?"

"I told him I'd forgotten my phone. He was there when the meeting broke up, so he'd seen me leave earlier. We chatted and walked back to the storeroom together while I retrieved the phone, then he walked me to the front door and I left."

"So he *can* vouch for you," Anne declared.

Wendy shook her head. "No, I already told you, I had already been in the museum for a little while before he saw me. It was only a minute or so, but he can't swear to that. Plus, I was carrying this big shoulder bag, so I could have already had the vase in there before he saw me. And for all he knows, I could have left the phone deliberately as an excuse to go back."

"Why were you carrying the bag in the museum?" Anne asked, though she immediately regretted it, fearing Wendy would feel that even Anne suspected her.

But Wendy just shrugged. "A matter of habit, I suppose. It was just the bag I had that day. I had several books to bring back here, and that was just the most convenient one. If I had a better reason to be carrying that bag that day, I'd probably look less suspicious. But I don't."

Anne felt a brief pang that the library had even the smallest part in Wendy's current troubles. "Well, who is this security guard, anyway?" she demanded, trying to take Wendy's mind off that point.

"His name is Theo," Wendy said. "But I only know his first name. Hal brought in several temporary security guards because of the auction. I think Miles Bridges helped recruit them. I'm sure the police were able to find out his last name easily enough, but I only know him as Theo." Wendy shrugged. "He seems like a nice enough guy. And I gather from the police that he corroborated everything I just told you. But he can't account for the entire time I was at the museum, which leaves space open for the police to have their suspicions."

Anne continued to buck up her friend's spirits, but it soon became clear that covering the same ground over and over was doing Wendy more harm than good, so eventually Anne said that she could handle the library and suggested that Wendy go home. If there was anything that was going to lift Wendy's spirits, thought Anne, it was her family. But after Wendy had left, Anne sat brooding on everything that Wendy had told her, and wondered if having her own little talk with Theo the security guard might be in order.

Anne was still deep in these reflections when Michael Banks dropped by the library. Once they finished exchanging greetings, Anne asked, "Do you think that security guard is telling us everything he knows?"

The police officer's brows drew together and his lips pursed. He looked at her for a few moments and then said, "What are you talking about, Anne?"

"Theo the security guard," she answered. "The guy who saw Wendy at the museum that night."

After a beat, Michael gave his head a resigned shake. "Why wouldn't he tell *us* everything he knows?"

His emphasis on the word *us* was not lost on her, and his subtle chastisement of her interference stung. Even so, she pressed on. "But he's so close to clearing her entirely from suspicion! If he had just seen her as soon as she walked into the museum…" She wanted to ask whether the security guard himself was a suspect, but the expression on Michael's face caused her to bite back the question. Instead, she meekly explained, "I've been talking with Wendy."

"So I see." The police officer passed a hand over his jaw. "Look, Anne, we've known each other a long time, and I'm very sorry that your friend has been caught up in this investigation, but you've got to trust us to do our jobs, okay?"

Contrite, Anne nodded.

"So," he continued after a moment, "I left you to talk with Stratton and Hollis yesterday on the way out of the station. Would you be willing to tell me what you said?"

Anne still felt the sting of being chastised, but she responded. "I invited them to come back to the library, but they couldn't, so

I made an appointment to go out and visit Mr. Stratton on Monday."

"Anne!" Michael exclaimed. "What are you doing?"

"He tried to make a very generous donation to the library," she responded defensively. "At the very least, I need to thank him for his intention. And who knows? Perhaps he's still willing to make one. I do have a responsibility to look out for the library's interests, you know."

Michael looked at her. What she'd said was true, even if it had not really been her priority when she made the appointment.

"I suppose," he said reluctantly but in a calmer tone. "But do this for me, Anne, okay? After you've talked with him, come by the station and tell me about it."

Surprised, Anne said, "Yes, of course." She regarded him thoughtfully for a moment. "I guess you didn't get anything out of him yourself?"

Michael ignored this. "So the reason I came by was to ask whether you had anyone come into the library prior to the theft and show unusual interest in the vase. Especially after the article ran in the newspaper."

"Well, sure, we had lots of people come in and ask about it," Anne said. "Many of them were under the impression that they could see it here, despite the article. But we directed them all down to the museum." She shrugged. "Many people seemed excited for the library, which was nice."

"But do any of those conversations stand out in particular?" Michael persisted. "Anyone who seemed unusually eager or curious? Or who struck you as odd in any way?"

Michael's questions jogged something in Anne's memory. "Oh my goodness!" she exclaimed. "There was the gentleman who wanted to buy the vase outright, before it ever went to the auction."

Michael gave her an annoyed, why-didn't-you-tell-me-this-sooner? look.

"I'm sorry," she continued quickly, "I wasn't actually here when he came in. It was the day after the newspaper story ran. Remi Miller told me about it. But he didn't leave a name or contact information or anything. And as far as I know, he never came back."

Chapter Fifteen

Sunday service attendance always declined somewhat with the arrival of summer weather, as people went on vacation or spent more time outdoors with their families, like Wendy and her family, who had left for their trip that weekend.

Anne always enjoyed services during the summer. They felt more relaxed and joyful, and at the coffee hour afterward, the women in sundresses and the men in polo shirts made for a more colorful gathering than in the colder months. The sunlight that streamed in through the windows didn't hurt, either.

Despite her concern for Wendy, Anne felt happy and content as she nibbled the coffee-hour refreshments. In addition to the fine weather, another reason for her good mood was relief. She had been dreading seeing Gertrude Haines this morning, but Gertrude was among the missing that day.

She had allowed Ben and Liddie to go outside and play on the church's swing set along with most of the other children who'd been to the service, and she drifted around the fellowship hall, catching up with people she hadn't talked with in a while. Much of the conversation focused on the upcoming Antique Appraisal Fair and Auction, which was now just two weeks away.

Helen Smith stepped away to replenish the refreshments on the table, and Anne stood alone at one end of the hall, gazing at the crowd and feeling more relaxed than she had in some time. She had just waved to Maggie Sloan across the room when Jana Bagwell stepped up. Anne didn't know Jana well, but she felt a certain kinship with her since she was also the mother of young children. Her three kids were probably out on the swing set with Ben and Liddie.

Anne greeted her with a smile, and they chatted about summer plans. Jana and her family were making a trip out west later in the summer to visit the Grand Canyon. Anne had hopes of getting down to Florida at some point to visit her parents but found it difficult to get away from the library for long trips, especially during the busy summer season. Now she felt guilty that she wasn't taking her own children to see the Grand Canyon.

Suddenly Jana riveted her full attention by saying, "So I guess you've had to take that display down."

"Excuse me?" Anne asked. As far as she knew, Jana and her children were not patrons of the library. She had never once seen them there that she could recall.

"You know," Jana said, though a note of doubt crept into her voice, "the one that Gertrude talked about in her letter."

"Oh, I see," Anne said, forcing herself to remain calm. "No, that display just went up. I generally leave them up for several weeks before changing to a new one. It's not time yet for that one to come down."

Jana now looked thoroughly confused. "But Gertrude's letter…"

Anne gave her a moment to finish her thought, but when Jana didn't continue, she said, "Of course, Gertrude is entitled to her opinion. But I don't happen to agree with her." She was trying to be firm and unambiguous without sounding defensive or critical.

"But if it's bad for children..." Jana had an almost plaintive note in her voice.

"If I had thought that was the case, I wouldn't have put the display up in the first place." She held Jana's gaze for a moment, and then she continued in a softer tone, "I think it's an important topic and that the display is perfectly appropriate for the age group."

Jana slunk off with a troubled look on her face.

Anne swallowed her rising anger. The idea that she would put up a display that was harmful or damaging to children was an insult to her status as both a mother and a librarian. It was an attack on two of the most fundamental aspects of her identity. After a moment, she closed her eyes and said a brief prayer for a calm heart and understanding mind. She wasn't mad at Jana, she realized, but at Gertrude Haines.

In an effort to distract herself, Anne made her way back to the refreshment table. She kept an eye out for Jana Bagwell, not wishing to encounter her again, but she seemed to have left. Slowly, Anne felt her equilibrium returning.

She was just collecting a second slice of some wonderful banana bread that Helen Smith had brought when she heard someone behind her mention Wendy Pyle's name and something about Wendy not being in church that day.

"Ah yes," said a man's voice with a chuckle, "I guess she has fled town for the time being."

Anne's anger came roaring back to life. Part of her realized that the remark had been meant as nothing more than a joke, but

Anne still had to restrain herself from giving him a piece of her mind. She knew she'd probably say something, but first she needed to recover enough self-control to do so civilly.

But before she could fully regain her composure, she heard Helen Smith's voice in tones of gentle admonishment say, "Now, David, that's uncalled for. Her family has been planning this trip for months."

"Yes, I know you're right," he replied. "It just seems so odd that anyone could suspect her in the first place. It's hard to take the idea seriously."

Feeling sheepish, Anne picked up her slice of banana bread and fled.

* * *

When the coffee hour was over, Anne stayed behind to help Helen clean up. When they were the last two people there, Anne mentioned that she had overheard the exchange and thanked Helen for speaking up.

"I was so upset," Anne said, "that I couldn't have stayed calm." She paused in stacking the dried plates and cups into the cabinets to offer a rueful smile.

Helen nodded. "I thought I saw your back stiffen." She returned the silverware to its drawer. "But David meant no harm. He doesn't believe for a moment that Wendy is guilty."

"I know," Anne said. "It's just that the whole thing has been so upsetting to her that I find myself rather sensitive on her behalf."

"Small towns thrive on rumors," Helen observed, "and the ones that cast someone in a bad light are the ones that people are quickest to believe and to spread, even when they ought to know better." She pulled out a length of plastic wrap from an industrial-sized dispenser and ran the blade across to slice it off. "Wendy understands that as well as anyone, though of course it's cold comfort when the rumor is about you." She gave Anne a reassuring smile. "But she'll get through it."

Anne replied, "That's what I keep telling her, but it's nice to hear it from somebody else."

Helen finished tucking the plastic wrap around the ends of an uncut loaf of her banana bread. "I always like to make sure there's plenty," she said, as if Anne had remarked on the leftover loaf. "I suppose I should put this in the freezer."

"It was delicious." Anne dried her hands on a towel and looked about for any remaining tasks.

Helen smiled and pushed the loaf along the counter toward her. "Why don't you take it then? It's always better fresh than frozen. You can give it to Ben and Liddie or perhaps put it out at the library."

Anne smiled. "Actually, I can think of someone else who might appreciate it."

* * *

When she returned home from church, Anne found an e-mail from Miles Bridges responding to her request for Percy Stratton's address. She looked at a map on the Internet and found that he lived on the outskirts of State College in a tiny settlement on the road to Blue Hill. Anne realized that it was an area she was somewhat familiar with. She had taken the kids to a nearby farm to go blueberry picking.

Using the satellite pictures online, she examined the area. Across the street from the farm, there were several scattered structures, but it was difficult to make out what they were. Anne thought that she recalled a barn or perhaps a derelict house being used as a barn. She thought there had also been a brick house, well back from the road, but the clusters of trees in the satellite images obscured much of her view.

Well, she figured, she'd find out when she got there.

* * *

She had arranged for all-day coverage at the library on Monday, so once she delivered Ben and Liddie to their friends' houses for playdates, she spent some time on household chores until it was time to grab Helen's banana bread and head in the direction of State College.

It was a beautiful morning to be out driving in the countryside. The trees were full and lush. Many flowers, both wild and domestic, were in bloom. The warmth of the season still had an element of freshness to it, even if the initial glad surprise of the spring thaw was long past.

Anne drove past broad fields and small wood lots, suburban homes, and well-kept lawns.

When she arrived at the crossroads where Percy Stratton's house was, she was surprised to find more structures clustered about than she recalled, as well as a larger stand of trees. In addition to the brick house set back from the road, there was a newer house she had forgotten completely. This darkened house had a For Sale sign in front of it. But the number on this house was not the one she wanted, and she decided that the brick house must be her destination.

She followed a long drive, carefully examining the house as she approached. It had a neglected and despondent air. Much of the building was covered in vines, and the brick façade seemed to be on the verge of crumbling. Several shutters were missing and others were askew. The drive itself was unpaved and rutted, with grass growing profusely down the center.

She parked before the front door and stepped from the car. The small porch sagged, and the condition of the wood suggested a degree of rot. She could see a corner of another porch that ran down one side of the house, and this appeared to be loaded with lumber, boxes, and perhaps old furniture.

Anne began to question her decision to visit Percy Stratton, but then she thought about Wendy, plucked up her courage, stepped up to the front door, and rang the bell.

She waited for some time, occasionally picking up odd and distant sounds from inside the house. At first she thought she heard voices, and it seemed that they were making their way toward the door, but no one arrived.

She was about to ring the bell again when suddenly the door opened and Mr. Stratton stood before her. While he had been neatly dressed at the police station, now he was clad in a stained flannel shirt and old workman's pants. And where his expression then had been mild and somewhat vacant, his eyes now glinted with greater awareness but also irritability.

He stood in the doorway and looked Anne up and down for a moment, and then muttered, "We don't want any." He began to turn away.

"Mr. Stratton," she called quickly, and the use of his name turned him back again.

"Eh?" he grunted.

"Mr. Stratton, it's me. Anne Gibson."

He peered at her more closely but with no sign of recognition. "Do I know you?" There was a note of hesitation and confusion in his voice, as if he realized there was a chance he should know her.

Slowly, Anne replied, "We met at the police station last week. You came with your nephew, Mr. Hollis, to talk with the police about the vase that was stolen." She felt that her words were registering, but it was difficult to tell how much.

"Yes," he said, "I was there. What about it?"

"We met then," Anne repeated. "I'm Anne Gibson. The librarian in Blue Hill. The library that you donated the vase to."

"The library," Mr. Stratton repeated. Apparently he decided to accept this because he looked at her again and said, "Well, what do you want?"

"When we met last week," Anne said, "we made an appointment for me to come visit you today."

Mr. Stratton chewed his lip for a moment but then gave a curt nod and turned back into the house, gesturing for her to follow.

Inside, he shuffled back against the wall and waited for Anne to pass, then closed the door behind her. He stepped around her, muttering, "You'd best come back to the porch."

They stood in a short hallway with a flight of stairs leading up to the second floor. The hallway was poorly lit, but it seemed to Anne that it was stuffed with stacks of boxes lined up along the wall. The ones on top looked precarious.

Mr. Stratton passed through a door on Anne's right, gesturing for her to follow. This led into a living room even more stuffed with boxes and furniture than the hall had been. Anne spotted a TV set in one corner with a ratty, overstuffed chair facing it from a few feet away. A tray table was placed next to the chair and appeared to hold a dirty bowl and coffee mug. The rest of the room was crammed with stuff. Anne suspected that behind the piles of newspapers and magazines and paper bags filled with more papers, she would find a couch and coffee table, for to one side, just poking out above a cascading stack of magazines and junk mail and crumpled candy wrappers, was the top of a lamp shade. The floor was completely covered with trash except for a path that led diagonally across the floor to another door.

Mr. Stratton led her along this path and they stepped into what Anne assumed was a dining room, though it was every bit as full of stuff as the living room had been. As they skirted the center mass, Anne took a guess at the dining room table she assumed lay under the clutter.

She noticed that scattered throughout the rooms they'd passed through, empty soup cans littered the floor. She wondered if Percy Stratton had been eating soup directly from the cans.

From the dining room, they passed into a kitchen that was not quite so packed with stuff, though still pretty cluttered by any normal standard, and then through the kitchen out onto a back porch, where a certain amount of space had been kept clear around a table with a few chairs.

Despite his age and infirmity, Mr. Stratton had led Anne fairly rapidly through the house. Now he stopped and turned to her, as if awaiting some comment or criticism.

All Anne could think to do was hold up the package she carried and say, "I thought you might like some banana bread."

Mr. Stratton's eyes lit up and his face betrayed the first trace of pleasure she'd seen since she arrived. "Well, well," he muttered, "well, well." He looked at her and said, "That's right nice of you Ms.…er, right nice. Why don't you…" He gestured in the direction of the table and chairs, and continued, "We'll have some, eh? You'll join me?"

"Thank you, Mr. Stratton," Anne said, speaking loudly and distinctly, "that would be very nice." She stepped over and settled herself into the chair on the far side of the table.

"Good, good," said Mr. Stratton. "Be right back."

He bustled back into the kitchen. Anne set about unwrapping the banana bread, and Mr. Stratton soon returned bearing a butter knife and two tumblers of water. Anne accepted hers with thanks, and though she noticed that the glass was not entirely clean, she said nothing as she set it down. The butter knife was not ideal for cutting the bread, but fortunately the loaf was still soft and moist. Anne cut a couple of slices and Mr. Stratton eagerly picked one up. He'd brought no plates.

Once they were each on their second slice, Anne noticed Mr. Stratton glancing at her shrewdly, apparently waiting to see what she would do next.

Chapter Sixteen

Anne took another slow bite of the banana bread, wishing to appear relaxed and unhurried. Casually she said, "I was sorry that we didn't have a chance to talk more when we met at the police station, Mr. Stratton. But I was glad to meet you and your nephew."

Mr. Stratton nodded at this but said nothing.

He seemed more alert and cognizant than he had at the station, but Anne was still unsure how much was registering. Did he remember her now? Did he even remember going to the police station?

"As I mentioned, I wanted to thank you for your generosity in donating the vase to the library. It's a shame that the vase was stolen, but that doesn't detract from your desire to help us."

Mr. Stratton merely nodded again, but the gleam had returned to his eye. Anne cut him another slice of the bread.

"Of course," she continued, "we were dying with curiosity when we first heard the news, since you acted anonymously. It was a very intriguing situation."

He chuckled with pleasure at this but otherwise kept his silence. She decided to pursue a different tack.

"When we spoke at the station, you mentioned my aunt Edie. Edie Summers. I'd be interested to hear how you knew her."

At last, Mr. Stratton gave her an approving wink. "Told you before, I *didn't* know her—except by reputation. But I knew she was a remarkable lady. I was really sad to learn of her passing and to realize I had waited too late to get to know her personally." He paused and seemed to be considering for a moment. "When I read about her arranging a library for Blue Hill, well, I thought that was a right smart thing. And I've been meaning to do something to help out for a while. It just took me a bit of time to get around to it. But then Miles was telling me about this auction you all are having over there, and that seemed like just the way to go about it. I didn't want to call attention to myself, you see, but Miles showed me how we could fix that up. Of course, we didn't expect it to become a police matter." To Anne's surprise, he chuckled as if someone had played a good joke on him.

"That was a shame, certainly, though I'm glad to know who our benefactor is."

Anne thought briefly about what she'd said to Michael Banks. Did she really have an obligation to see if this man was still willing to give something else to the library? In her heart of hearts, Anne suspected that this was what she ought to do, but somehow, she just couldn't bring herself to broach the subject. After all, he had already lost a very valuable possession, even if he *had* meant to give it away.

Instead, she found herself asking, "I'd be interested to hear about your vase, Mr. Stratton. Are you a collector?"

Mr. Stratton leaned back in his chair and said, "No, no. Not me. But I was in the war, you see, the Pacific theater, and I was there for the occupation. And you know, all the boys were doing it, picking up little souvenirs to take home. Or big ones, sometimes.

And the people over there, they needed money and friends more than they needed things. They were happy to sell off valuable items at good prices."

He fell silent, and Anne said, "I imagine you could find some nice things, if you knew what to look for."

Mr. Stratton shook his head. "I weren't no expert. But I had a friend, Eddie, and he knew all about this stuff. It was in the family business in some way."

"And Eddie was willing to help you?" Anne suggested.

"I saved Eddie's life once, and we stayed good friends after. So we'd go out on leave, and go around and look at what all people had for sale. And Eddie'd pick up a lot of stuff and then tell me about it later. Real good stuff, and he'd send it back to his family. But every once in a while, he'd say, 'Hey, Perce, that's a nice looking vase there. You ought to think about buying that.' And I'd take the hint and he'd helped me dicker a good price. And that's how I come to have them vases."

"Vases?" Anne asked. "So you have a collection?"

Mr. Stratton shrugged. "If you want to call it that. I got a bunch, anyway. And a few years after the war, I had a fella look at 'em for me, and it turned out ole Eddie had steered me right every time, and more than right in a few cases, if you know what I mean. So the missus and I, we figured we'd hang on to them and enjoy 'em, and then someday, you know, they'd help us out in our retirement.

"And then Marie, well..." Mr. Stratton's shoulders slumped and his gaze lost some focus. "In the end, I just never did anything with them. They sat around the house collecting dust. So when Miles told me about this benefit auction, I figured I could put at least one of 'em to good use." His gaze refocused on Anne. " 'Cept it didn't quite work out, and I'm sorry for that."

"As I say," Anne replied, "we're still very grateful that you thought of us."

Mr. Stratton narrowed his eyes and pursed his lips, then after a moment he nodded and said, "Well, now, so tell me about this library. Is it doing well?"

Mr. Stratton seemed genuinely interested, and Anne ended up giving him a fairly detailed account of setting up the library and the programs and goals she had created for it. He said little, but every now and then he asked a shrewd question. As she often did when talking about the library, Anne found herself growing enthusiastic, and she tried not to get tiresome. But Mr. Stratton's interest showed no sign of slackening.

After she had gone on for some time, Anne finally blurted out a question that had nagged her for a while. "But why Blue Hill, Mr. Stratton? I mean, I don't begrudge anyone a good opinion of my aunt, but still, you live down here."

"Oh, but I grew up in Blue Hill," Mr. Stratton said quickly. "Me and Marie both did. And even though we ended up down the road here, we always thought we'd move back someday." He stopped abruptly and then added, "But we never did."

"I'm sorry," Anne said, observing the extent of his grief after all these years. She wondered briefly whether her own loss would still be that raw and painful so many years from now. To change the subject, she continued, "Well, your nephew seems to feel that you're quite rooted here."

A grim smile formed on his lips. "Oh, Ronnie's a good boy, but he don't think I can look after myself anymore. Seems to think I need watching." He sighed. "Maybe he's got a point. I know there's some days when I'm not as sharp as I once was." He glanced shyly at Anne but then said with more vehemence, "But that don't mean I need to go to a home!"

Anne wasn't quite sure what to say. She had no wish to pry, but finally, she said, "Is that..."

"Oh yes," Mr. Stratton said. "He's got some place out there near Pittsburgh all picked out." And then in a low, defeated tone, he added, "I agreed to go look at it."

They sat in silence for a minute, until finally Mr. Stratton lifted his head and said, "So, young lady, did you want to see my collection?"

* * *

The vases were housed in a large cabinet on the far side of the dining room. Amid all the clutter, Anne hadn't noticed it when he'd led her through before, but she saw now that when the room was tidy, the display of vases must have been quite impressive. Now, however, they had to share their shelf space with other miscellaneous items that appeared to have been stuck there haphazardly.

Mr. Stratton owned around twenty vases of various sizes, styles, and colors – some Asian, some Parisian, some Egyptian or from the Middle East, from all around the world, truth be told. "We liked havin' them around," he said, a touch of pride in his voice. "'Course they ain't all valuable like that one was. I was always told that was the best of the collection. Couple others come close, but most are just nice to look at, you know? As I say, we just liked havin' them."

They gazed at the shelves for a bit, and then Mr. Stratton pointed to a small gap. "The one I gave the library always sat here." He pointed at another. "And then this one here was always Marie's favorite."

But then he stopped abruptly and his face grew very troubled. "Wait," he said, "or was it..." His eyes anxiously scanned the shelves. "Or was it this one?" His finger rested lightly on another vase one shelf down. "I don't...something's not..." He hung his head and seemed to shrink into himself. "I can't even tell anymore," he said in a small voice. "I can't remember which one it was."

He seemed on the verge of tears, and Anne's heart went out to him. "I'm sure she wouldn't mind," Anne said. "You've honored her memory in so many ways."

Mr. Stratton looked up but didn't really seem to see her.

"Come on, Mr. Stratton," Anne said, "let's have one last slice of banana bread."

She led him back out onto the porch but struggled for something to say.

"Have you...," she fumbled, "have you had the vases regularly appraised over the years?"

Mr. Stratton seemed to have recovered his self-possession, and he mechanically accepted the piece of bread Anne handed to him. He shook his head at the question, and said, "No, no. Just that one time. No need after that. The fella who did it that one time used to call me up every once in a while to ask if I still had them. And years ago other people would ask about them sometimes too—folks we'd just shown them to or whatever. But I've not had anybody asking about them for years and years. 'Cept that one gal the other day." He gave her a watery smile. "That's what I get for lettin' them out of the house again."

"What do you mean?" Anne asked.

"Well, it was that gal that works with Miles, wasn't it?" he replied. "Even though I told him to keep my identity a secret, I guess he told her, because she turned up one day with some other fella, askin' if she could have a look at 'em." He winked at Anne. "She was another one for callin' them a collection. Funny though," he added musingly, "when I asked him later, Miles said he hadn't told her my name at all."

Anne cocked her head. "But she said she worked with him? What was her name?"

Percy Stratton frowned for a few moments then shook his head. "No," he said, "I can't recall it. She told me, but I just can't remember. The other fella, she didn't even get to introduce him." He began to cackle at the memory. "I sent them right off. Sent them packing. They didn't even get past the front door."

But while Mr. Stratton enjoyed the memory of running them off, Anne was deep in thought. Finally, she asked, "Was her name Angie, by any chance? Angie Staub?"

Percy Stratton paused as if listening to the name in his head for a moment, and then a smile of recognition slowly spread across his features.

"You're a regular mind reader, Ms. Gibson," he said. "That was it exactly."

Chapter Seventeen

Anne spent the next morning going about her tasks at the library with an ever-increasing sense of foreboding. Her encounter with Jana Bagwell at coffee hour had rattled her. She had previously been secure in her sense that Gertrude Haines's opinion was a minority view and that most people who examined the question would agree with Anne.

But Jana Bagwell had reminded her that many people wouldn't examine the question for themselves. Many would simply see that there was a letter in the newspaper and assume that it must have a valid point. They wouldn't necessarily apply their own critical analysis.

Anne had not yet encountered any other people who assumed Gertrude must be right, but she'd been away from the library for most of Monday. What was making her nervous now was a program scheduled in the afternoon that would bring in half a dozen women, some of whom might also assume that Anne should give in to the first sign of criticism.

The program was long-planned and had nothing to do with the display or even with children's books. In fact, it was related to Railroad Days and the upcoming Antique Appraisal Fair and Auction. But still, it was the first public program she'd had since the letter had run in last week's paper, and she wondered if there would be any further pushback about the display.

Whenever she had a quiet moment, she sat at her desk, took some deep breaths, and tried to prepare herself, though she wasn't really sure what she would say. She drew a piece of paper toward her and began to brainstorm some points that she would want to make if the occasion arose.

She had grown absorbed in this task and lost track of the time, when suddenly the door opened and all six women entered together. There had been a certain amount of laughter and chatter from the group as the door opened, but as soon as they were all inside, they quieted and seemed to turn as one to look at Anne.

Anne offered her best smile in greeting.

Before she could say anything, Coraline Watson called out, "Anne Gibson, I have a bone to pick with you!"

Anne struggled to maintain a polite smile, but her heart sank.

"*Why* haven't you put those fabulous nesting dolls on display?"

Anne blinked in surprise. "What?"

"Remi Miller showed them to me yesterday," Coraline explained once Anne had led the group into the room where they were to meet. "They're gorgeous."

"Don't worry," Anne said with a relieved laugh. "I'm planning a display for them after the appraisal fair."

Today's program was about research resources for collectibles and antiques. After all, people couldn't take the entire contents of their attics to the appraisal fair, so they needed to know how to look things up on their own as well. Given the interest generated by the Railroad Days events, Anne's sign-up sheet for the program had quickly filled.

She knew that a considerable part of the class would be taken up with each participant showing off what she intended to take to the appraisal fair, but that was fine. Those would all serve as good examples to work with. Anne had directed participants to show up with something that they wanted to research, and Anne herself had set out her collection of nesting dolls to use as examples if necessary. Which was how Remi Miller had been able to show them to Coraline the day before.

It appeared, however, that she wouldn't lack for examples. Every woman present was carrying one or even two shopping bags, and they placed these now on the long conference table and began to unload them. Soon they were all elbow deep in the heirlooms and curiosities that the ladies had brought.

After each woman took turns introducing her items—everything from a book of Robert Frost's poems to a stamp collection to old train lanterns—Anne smiled and clapped her hands. The variety of items was going to be a challenge, but she'd been leading budding researchers through the wealth of reference material for years. It was time to get started.

* * *

Anne returned from her program in high spirits. On her desk, she found a message from Remi asking her to return a call from Grace Hawkins. Rather than let her imagination run riot, she picked up the phone right away and dialed the news editor's number.

"Anne!" Grace said in a cheerful tone, which quickly grew more serious as she continued, "I'm glad you called. Listen, I don't make a habit of alerting people to what's going to be in the paper...but I thought I should give you a heads-up that there will be some more letters in tomorrow's edition about your column."

"Letters?" Anne asked. "Plural?"

"Well, about your column and perhaps even more about the letters that ran last week. Or especially, the critical one."

"Are they rushing to my defense, by any chance?" Anne chuckled, but she couldn't completely mask her nervousness.

There was a pause while Grace apparently tried to sort out whether Anne was being serious or ironic. Then she said brightly, "Some. But others, not so much."

Anne sighed. "I see. That bad, is it?"

"I didn't say it was bad," Grace quickly retorted.

"But you've broken your usual policy to call and warn me about them."

"That's just because you seemed surprised last time. And because you seemed to think that there wouldn't be any more."

Anne smiled to herself. "So you're calling to tell me 'I told you so'?" she teased.

"No, of course not. I just thought you should be aware. Also, I thought I'd ask again if you want to write a response."

Anne thought about this. "I guess that will depend on what they actually say. If it's just a matter of dissenting opinions, well, everyone has that right. But if there's a bigger issue and I could contribute to a discussion, or if there's been some misunderstanding that should be cleared up, well, I might consider it." Having worked out her own thoughts, she added, "What's your advice?"

"I don't advise anything," Grace said. "I think you have the correct perspective on the situation, so it will be up to you." After a moment, she added, "You know, I realize this might seem like a drag, but in fact, I think it's a good thing. It shows that people are interested in what you have to say and in what goes on at the library. I think this bodes well for your monthly column."

Anne laughed out loud. "Well, thank you, I think. Though I have to say I hope future columns do not give me so much heartburn!"

Chapter Eighteen

The next morning, the brand new edition of the *Blue Hill Gazette* sat neatly folded on Anne's desk as she glared down at it in annoyance.

The annoyance was not with the paper but with herself. Normally, reading the paper was the first thing she did when it came out each week, but today she'd been staring at it for several minutes, reluctant to open it and read the letters Grace had told her about.

Above the fold, the *Gazette's* front page featured an account of the latest meeting of the city council, though Anne knew without reading the story that it likely contained little surprising information. There was also a story about the latest developments in a long-running dispute over a piece of land that was barely within the borders of the town. It appeared that the parties involved had finally agreed to put it into conservation easement.

Anne reached for the paper and flipped it over so that she could what was below the fold. She was happy to see an interesting account of Hal McCollum and his oral history project. He had already been conducting interviews at the museum and elsewhere, but the big push was scheduled for the Antique Appraisal Fair and Auction, when many people would be gathered in one place. Since that was coming up soon, this article was well-timed to generate interest and get people thinking about participating.

As Anne became drawn into the story, she unfolded the paper so that she could follow the story when it jumped to an inside page. Anne figured that getting the paper open constituted progress, though she still read the story to its very last word before she thought again about turning back to the letters.

Finally, she took a deep breath and flipped to the back of the paper, where the editorials, letters, and commentary were.

She was surprised to find that there were seven letters about her column and the earlier responses. Even after Grace's call, this was more than she'd expected.

At first, she could only concentrate enough to give them a quick scan. There seemed to be three on her side and four against. She chastised herself for even thinking in terms of "sides," but she found it difficult to rid herself of the notion completely.

She closed her eyes, said a quick prayer for an understanding heart, and then settled down to read the letters carefully. She began with those she thought were critical in order to get the worst out of the way first.

One thing that quickly became clear was that the writers of the critical letters did not seem to have actually been to the library to see the display. Two of them admitted as much and the other two made comments that were inconsistent with having actually viewed the display. They all seemed simply to take as a given Gertrude Haines's view that the photographs in the display were inappropriate for children.

In fact, two of the letters had almost nothing to do with the display or Anne's column whatsoever. They simply took the complaint that Haines had made as an occasion to rant about what they saw as the increasing level of violence in popular culture—movies and television came in for particular condemnation—and a general coarsening of American life. These letters did not engage with the historical or social significance of Anne's display whatsoever. She recognized them as the work of people prepared to mount their own particular hobbyhorses at the slightest provocation.

The other two letters struck a more hysterical "think of the children" tone. This was a tactic that Anne tended to resent as both a librarian and a mother. It was, after all, in both her nature and her training to "think of the children." That was why she had written the column and created the display to begin with. When people invoked this kind of unspecified potential harm to children, Anne usually saw it as a way to make an emotional run around any actual discussion or logic.

The authors of both of these letters made a point of saying that they would not take their children to the library while the display was up. As it happened, these were people who did not take their children to the library anyway. Each family had been in once and gotten a library card, and then never returned. But the library was meant to serve the community, and this kind of public pronouncement might discourage other potential patrons as well.

No matter how right Anne might be, if the library was empty, then she was failing both Blue Hill and her aunt.

Hoping for some consolation, Anne turned to the letters of support.

One was from Wendy, who had found time to write even while preparing for a family trip and struggling with her own personal distress. Anne felt a surge of gratitude well up for her friend's support even in a time of trouble for herself.

The letter, however, was more a tribute to the library and to Anne than it was an engagement with the complaints that Gertrude Haines had made. Wendy wrote that she "took exception to certain criticisms" that had been made of the library and its librarian and then went on to praise both as valuable additions to the Blue Hill community. Anne didn't really think of herself as an "addition," but many of the *Gazette's* readers would be unaware that she'd grown up in Blue Hill.

Anne was surprised and gratified to find that the next letter was from someone she didn't even know. It was someone who had taken the trouble of coming to the library and seeing the display, however, because the letter contained a moving account of its author's response to the photographs and books, as well as some reflections on Dr. King's historical significance. Though she recognized that she was biased, Anne found this letter much more thoughtful and better informed than the critical ones.

The final letter was from Maggie Sloan, and this was a full-throated defense of the importance of knowing and teaching the historical record, both the good and the bad, to children and indeed to all citizens. She quoted George Santayana's well-known lines, "Those who cannot remember the past are condemned to repeat it," declaring that it was the responsibility of adults in general, and of libraries as institutions, to ensure that the young are able to learn from and avoid the mistakes of the past.

Maggie expressed sympathy for those who wished to protect the young from unpleasant or upsetting information. But such an impulse, while understandable, was in fact often a failure of our responsibility toward children. To coddle children, she said, was to fail to prepare them for the hard knocks of life.

These words stirred Anne's memories of Aunt Edie, who had frequently said the same thing. Setbacks and disappointments were the lot of all people, Aunt Edie maintained, and children who were sheltered from the minor shocks of youth would never develop the resources to endure the larger tragedies that life would inevitably deliver from time to time.

"I've lived a very fortunate life myself," she would tell Anne. "Nobody knows it better. But I've had misfortunes like anyone, and the experience just makes me appreciate the good things all the more." The smile that she would give Anne when she said this had made Anne feel sure that she herself was one of those good things.

The library was empty and quiet, and these thoughts of Aunt Edie sent Anne far down the road of reminiscence, the newspaper and its letters, both for and against, forgotten for a time.

* * *

When the Miller twins arrived at the library later that day to help out, they found Anne scribbling on a pad of yellow paper but regularly ripping off the sheets, wadding them up, and tossing them into an overflowing wastebasket.

"What are you writing, Mrs. Gibson?" asked Remi with interest.

Anne looked up with her pen poised over the pad but then slowly relaxed and set it down. "I thought," she said, "that I should send a response to these letters after all." She gestured with the pen toward her desk, but the newspaper had gotten buried under books and other papers. Undeterred, she continued, "When I read them this morning, so many thoughts went racing through my mind. Objections, counterarguments, clarifications—or even agreements." She looked down at her pad. "It all seemed so clear, then. And Grace even suggested I consider writing a response. But then, when I set out to write it..."

Anne typically had little trouble putting her thoughts in writing. But on this occasion, whenever she started, she somehow couldn't avoid sounding judgmental or pompous or sanctimonious. None of these were adjectives that she wanted to apply to herself.

Perhaps, she thought, a fresh perspective would help start her down the right road.

"What did you think, Remi?"

Remi glanced desperately about for her sister, but Bella had already headed up the stairs. "About what?" she asked uncertainly.

"About all these letters in the paper," Anne said, gesturing toward the still buried *Gazette*. When this didn't seem to strike an immediate spark, she added, "About my column."

"You write a column?" Remi asked. "What's it about?"

Anne regarded Remi steadily for two long beats, but just as the girl was starting to get nervous again, she sighed inwardly and said, "It's about books and the library. I guess you're not much of a newspaper reader?"

"Nah," said Remi, shaking her head.

"Not even the online version?" Anne asked, now really curious.

Remi shook her head again. "Maybe I could follow them on Twitter?" she wondered.

Chapter Nineteen

The next morning, while Ben and Liddie were getting dressed, Anne let Hershey out into the backyard. The brilliant blue sky held the promise of an absolutely perfect day, and she longed to spend every available moment outside. She stood at the base of their private entrance staircase and watched as Hershey dashed from tree to tree, sniffing and barking at squirrels. His energetic activity reminded Anne of her own efforts to sniff out some scrap of information or insight that would definitely clear Wendy from suspicion in the theft of the stolen vase.

Her efforts so far hadn't been very productive, and she was growing concerned that soon she would simply have no time to spend on the project. As she cast about for some next step she could take, nothing came to mind.

Her conversation with Percy Stratton had shed some light on his own situation and how he came to own the vase in the first place, but she had never gotten a good answer out of him as to why he had chosen the library to be the recipient of his donation.

As she'd promised, Anne had called Michael Banks and described her visit with Mr. Stratton in as much detail as she could remember. But she didn't think she was able to provide him with much in terms of new information that would help the investigation. She had hoped that the interview would yield some good news to share with Wendy on her return.

Though it seemed like retracing old ground, the only active step she could think to take was to visit Miles Bridges again.

Since Midtown Antiques didn't open until ten, Anne had time to get the kids over to the babysitter at Alex's house, open the library, and make sure the volunteers had what they needed before she dashed off. She hoped to be at the shop just as the doors opened.

When she arrived at the shop, a display of brightly colored fiesta ware in the window was tantalizing, but Anne resisted the urge to prowl around the store. She went directly to the building next door and asked the clerk to let Miles Bridges know she was there.

"Oh dear..." The young clerk flipped through an appointment book and looked up at Anne with a flustered air. "Um, I don't see your name here in the calendar, and Mr. Bridges is out. Oh, we must have made a mistake..."

"No mistake," Anne said hurriedly. "I didn't have an appointment. I simply hoped to have a brief word with Mr. Bridges this morning before he got too busy."

The young clerk bit her lip and thought for a moment. "You're from the library, right? Well, Angie Staub is here. Perhaps she can help you?"

Anne nodded. She hadn't counted on a private talk with Angie, but perhaps Anne could get the young appraiser to open up to her. She quickly made a mental list of new questions. She remembered that her last meeting with Angie Staub had been brief and somewhat unpleasant, though Anne was willing to give the appraiser the benefit of the doubt. After all, the disappearance of a valuable antique, and one which could conceivably have been considered to be in the shop's care, must be distressing.

Anne was so deep in thought that she didn't hear Angie approach until the appraiser offered a quiet "ahem."

Anne turned and smiled broadly. "Ms. Staub, I'm sorry I didn't make an appointment, but I appreciate your time."

Angie smiled and beckoned Anne to follow her back to a work area, explaining that this was space that Miles had set aside for the use of the visiting appraisers who were assisting with the Blue Hill event. Unlike Miles's office, where the clutter seemed a reflection of his interests, the clutter here was simply the result of multiple people sharing a small space. It was crammed with reference books piled on every surface, and Angie had to remove a stack from the one visitor's chair for Anne to sit down. As she looked around, Anne saw numerous pictures of Asian ceramics thumbtacked to the wall.

"Before the donation of the vase," Anne began, "I had no idea how much there is to know about Chinese ceramics."

Angie, for once, smiled. "The history of China and all of Asia is so fascinating. That's what drew me to specialize in the vases, I think. The vases are beautiful, but once you understand how they reflect the dynasty they came from, you start to understand so much more about the culture and really start to see the artistry."

Anne leaned in. "I'm curious about the second vase. Have you been able to learn any more about it?"

Angie turned around and pulled up a picture of the vase on her computer. "It's a pattern called Famille Verte, from the Kangxi period in the seventeenth and early eighteenth century." She paused while Anne processed the dates, then added, "Except we can't verify its age from just the pictures."

"Are you suggesting that this could be a fake?"

Angie smiled. "If it's a fake, it's a good fake, and it's probably a hundred years old or more." She sighed. "*Fake* is probably the wrong word. *Exportware* better categorizes it. Produced to satisfy a growing trade with Europe and a newfound European taste for Chinese vases. These one-of-a-kind pieces were sold to Westerners as authentic 'Ming' vases. They weren't, but they were still made with skill and attention to detail and hand-painted by artists."

Angie paused and leaned back from the computer, absentmindedly rubbing her hand over her chin. "Of course," she said, "as I told Miles and that police officer, I estimate the value of this one to be about eight to ten thousand dollars." She smiled ruefully and crossed her legs.

"But at an auction in a small town like Blue Hill, that vase—or the original vase, for that matter—might go for a lot less than what a house like Christie's would get, right?" asked Anne.

"That's possible. Though serious collectors have their ways of finding out what's coming down the pike."

"How?"

"It's all in relationships. Knowing the dealers, who's knowledgeable. That sort of thing."

"That reminds me," Anne ventured. "The library had a strange visit from someone shortly before the vase was switched. Could that have been one of these collectors?"

Anne described the man as Remi had described him to her. As she spoke, she watched Angie's jaw tighten and her gaze shift to a far corner of the room.

"I don't know," Angie said curtly, cutting off Anne's description. "And I couldn't tell you if he were a client of mine. I respect the privacy of my clients. I take that *very* seriously."

Her tone of voice started to grow a little shrill, and her hands were clasped tightly in her lap. Anne must have trod on a sensitive subject, because Angie had gone from relaxed and informative to tightly wound in a matter of seconds.

"Well," Anne said, getting up, "I must get back to the library. You've been most helpful."

She extended her hand, and Angie had to disentangle her own to shake it.

* * *

Driving home, Anne felt that she might finally be closer to puncturing one of the veils of mystery surrounding the vases. Based on the rapid and extreme change in Angie's demeanor, Anne was convinced that Angie knew the identity of the strange visitor to the library.

Had Angie alerted some of her contacts or collectors about the vase? Had one of them come to Blue Hill without her knowledge? And if so, why would she be upset about that?

The angry blast of a horn from a passing car brought Anne's attention back to the road. She'd been going thirty miles an hour in a fifty zone. Slightly shaken, Anne pulled over at a nearby gas station and rummaged through her purse for anything on which to write a few notes.

On the back of an envelope she wrote, *A.S. has access to vases and contacts among collectors.* Then she took a calming breath and pulled back onto the road.

Anne got back to the library a little before lunch, typically a quiet time of day, so she turned to her computer and started her own research on Chinese vases. She was immediately overwhelmed with search results, many of which seemed highly suspicious.

After a few moments' thought, she narrowed her search to information about vases and Angie Staub. This yielded a much more manageable set of results, many of them articles that Angie had written.

On one of the more academic sites in her results, Anne was interested to find an article about "exportware" and the trade with Europe, coauthored by Angie and a man named Ambrose Carron. An accompanying photograph showed the two of them together, and the author bio described Carron as a "collector."

Before Anne could settle in and read the article, though, the library door opened and Alex Ochs strode through. With a flourish, he deposited a stack of books on the counter.

"There," he said triumphantly, "I beat the due date for once."

Anne laughed and sent her article to the printer before she turned to Alex and his books. "So have you nailed yourself to any more houses?"

"Not yet, but tomorrow's another day."

The printer started up with a racket, and Alex swiveled around to grab the pages for Anne as she dealt with his books.

"What's next on your reading list, Alex?" Anne asked, focused on logging in the returned books. But she was met with silence. When she looked up, she found Alex reading her printout on the vase.

"Hey!" He set the article down on the counter with the last page facing up. "I saw this guy at the railroad museum when I was doing some work there. He was looking at the vase. *The* vase."

Anne took a second look at the picture, then turned back to her computer, where the article was still on the screen, and clicked on Ambrose Carron's photo to make it larger.

"That's him," Alex said excitedly. "He even spoke to me. Asked about building a specialized shipping crate."

Chapter Twenty

After Alex left, Anne resumed her research with renewed determination, now focusing on Ambrose Carron. After feeling stymied in her desire to help Wendy for so long, Anne seized the clue, determined to wring every possible ounce of information out of it.

She quickly found more articles that Carron had written, all focused on Chinese ceramics. However, little biographical information accompanied these articles, and he appeared to have coauthored only the one with Angie Staub. He was variously described as an "expert," a "connoisseur," or a "collector," but no other information was given about him.

He didn't appear to be a scholar, or at least he wasn't affiliated with any university. Anne developed a list of half a dozen or so galleries that were known for handling the most important items in the field of Chinese ceramics, but he didn't seem to work for any of those either. She found no records of his participation in any major auctions in the area, though she got the impression that, like Angie, all the other dealers in this world were extremely discreet about their clients.

Nor was she able to find any information on him apart from his expertise in Asian ceramics, or at least none that she could definitively connect to him. The name appeared to belong to several people, to Anne's surprise, but she couldn't figure out which one was her man. She had strong suspicions about the one who lived in Manhattan, but she couldn't be sure. Nor was she even sure that the several Ambrose Carrons who seemed connected to other parts of the country were truly different individuals.

For a while, Anne wondered if "Ambrose Carron" was a pseudonym used just for articles, but she decided this was unlikely. She couldn't imagine that he would be able to publish articles on such a specialized topic unless the editors of the publications were convinced of his own expertise. And in such a small world, she didn't see how this could be the case without the author also being personally known to the editors.

The Internet could find you a lot of data, Anne reflected, but it sometimes did a lousy job of helping you turn that data into information.

She shook her head, dissatisfied. She had reached the limit of what publicly available information could tell her about Carron, but she resolved to take what she had learned to the police next day. After all, they had access to other sources of information and they might be able to learn a good deal more about him than she had.

But first, she had one more source of information of her own to tap.

* * *

Remi Miller entered the library the next morning juggling an awkward stack of books and not really looking where she was going. She had stopped to empty the overnight book return bin on her way in, which was one of her regular responsibilities when working the morning shift. There had been more returns than usual in the box, and she was already trying to glance at the spines and see what she had.

She nearly dropped the entire stack when she looked up to find Anne standing directly before her.

"Mrs. G?" she asked uncertainly.

Without speaking, her face tense with expectation, Anne held up a piece of paper.

Remi stared at the picture on the paper with a blank expression, but then slowly, recognition seemed to dawn. "Wait," she said after a moment, "wait, that's...that's him!"

"The man who wanted to buy the vase?"

"Yeah, that's him," Remi repeated with growing excitement. "That's...how did you do that? How did you find him?"

Anne mastered her triumphant smile and tried to look wise as she intoned, "Research."

* * *

When she arrived at the police station, Anne was surprised to find Michael Banks standing in the lobby, deep in conversation with Miles Bridges. Neither paid much attention to her at first, merely giving her a brief nod as they continued their conversation.

Miles said, "I appreciate these extra precautions, Officer Banks. With the theft of the vase and all..."

Michael shrugged. "Stealing something when the museum is closed is very different from walking off with it in the middle of the auction. The attending crowds are going to provide you better protection than we are."

"But there's something to be said for the effect of seeing numerous police officers about," Miles replied eagerly. "Not just to deter thieves but to reassure the attendees."

"Well, then I guess they will be very reassured," said Michael with a smile, "because we'll be there in force."

They had both adjusted their stances to include Anne in the conversation, and now they turned toward her.

Miles was the first to speak. "Anne, I'm so sorry I missed you yesterday. I wasn't expecting you, and I had to go out and evaluate the contents of a house for a possible estate sale. I think Angie met with you? I hope she was able to answer your questions."

At this, Michael's expression turned more quizzical, bordering on annoyed. He raised his eyebrows but refrained from speaking.

Flustered, Anne said, "Why . . . yes, yes, she did." She stopped, uncertain how to proceed.

After a moment, Michael asked, "How can I help you, Anne?"

Anne wondered if she should share her news with Miles present, but since it involved one of his hired experts, she felt he had the right to know. "Do you remember I told you about the mysterious stranger? The one who came to the library and asked about buying the vase outright?"

At the mention of "buying," Miles looked interested.

Michael nodded. "Sure, but we've had no luck tracking him down. You said he didn't leave any contact information, and though I got a description from Remi Miller, I wasn't able to make an identification." He turned to Miles. "You said you didn't know him."

Miles hemmed a bit. "Yes, but it was a rather vague description."

Michael conceded the point with another nod and turned back to Anne. "Why? What about him? Has he returned?"

"No," she replied, "but I think I know who he is."

She explained how her conversation with Angie Staub had set her searching for the expert's own published work, how she had come across Ambrose Carron, and how she had found that the two of them had even written an article together. Then she explained about Alex recognizing Carron's photograph, and about Remi's subsequent confirmation.

When she was finished, Miles Bridges looked grave and shook his head. "I'm sorry, Anne, but I think you must have misunderstood Angie. All of the appraisal consultants have specifically promised not to give their own clients any preferential treatment." He paused and seemed to be considering his own statement. "Of course, if something worthwhile turns up, we certainly want them to alert their networks. That just helps drive interest in the auction. But if you're suggesting that there was any improper collusion between Angie and a client, well, I can't believe that."

But Michael Banks looked interested. "Nevertheless, Mr. Bridges, whenever an individual has shown a particular interest in an article that is later stolen, that becomes something I need to look into." He gave the antiques dealer a determined look.

"Well, yes, I can quite understand that," Miles said, rapidly backing down.

"Besides," Michael continued, "I don't think what Anne has said necessarily points to anything improper. The vase got a lot of attention, and if Ms. Staub simply alerted someone who might be interested, well, that's one of the reasons that she's here, right? By itself, that doesn't suggest any collusion." But as he spoke, he smiled a strange, sly smile. "Of course, I'll need to come out and talk with Ms. Staub about this. Find out if she did indeed speak to this Mr. Carron and try to determine the nature and extent of his interest."

There seemed to be something unspoken behind his words, and Anne puzzled over what it could be. It wasn't until after she had left the station that a thought struck her.

Apparently, Michael had asked Miles about the mysterious stranger and had used the description that Remi had provided. Miles didn't know the man and had said so. But had Michael asked the same question of Angie Staub? And if so, had she also denied knowing the stranger?

And if she had, was it simply that the description was too vague? Or was it because she was hiding her acquaintance with Carron?

* * *

Anne's mind was filled with this possibility as she returned to the library and got back to work. Between this tantalizing question and a deeper satisfaction at finally having achieved some step that might help Wendy, Anne found her interest in the theft of the vase revitalized.

Mildred Farley arrived a few minutes later for her volunteer shift.

Anne greeted her warmly and said, "Thanks again, Mildred, for your flexibility about volunteering. I just don't know if Wendy is going to feel like coming in after they've been away on vacation.

I'm sure she'll have plenty of things at home that she'll need to attend to."

Anne had a mental picture of the laundry that could pile up when a family of nine went on vacation. She did not mention, but both understood, the additional strain that Wendy faced because of her status as a "suspect" in the theft.

"That's perfectly fine, dear," said Mildred, digging into a plastic bag that she'd carried in. "I'm happy to do it. And I need to give you this." She withdrew a book she was ready to return and handed it to Anne. It was the latest in a very long-running series of mystery novels. "I don't think the last few have been as good," she said in a confidential tone, as if the author might somehow overhear and take offense, "but I still hope for a return to form in the next one."

Anne nodded. She felt much the same way herself. As she checked the book back in, Mildred noisily folded up the plastic grocery bag and stowed it away inside a canvas tote bag she was also carrying.

Before Anne could ask what the second bag contained, Mildred looked at her brightly and said, "What have you decided to do about the newspaper?"

Anne grimaced. "I'm still having trouble coming up with a response," she admitted. "Back when I thought I wouldn't write an answer, I had all kinds of ideas. Now that I actually want to do so, though, I can't seem to get my thoughts organized and coherent."

"I'm sure it will come," Mildred said. "You always express yourself so well. You sound like your great-aunt Edie at times."

Anne smiled with real pleasure at this compliment. "Thank you! Though the truth is I haven't put much time into trying to write a response. I've been distracted again by Wendy's situation." And since she felt like talking about it, and since Mildred was a sympathetic listener, Anne told her about her talk with Angie Staub and the discovery of Ambrose Carron.

"You've accomplished quite a bit!" Mildred said. "Perhaps with more research, you'll be able to find out who the donor was as well."

Anne realized it had been a long time since she had discussed the whole situation with Mildred. "Oh, but we do know that!" she exclaimed. "I'm so sorry, I guess I never told you that part.'"

"That's all right, dear," Mildred said placidly. "You can tell me now."

"Miles Bridges arranged for the donor to go in and speak with the police. And they very kindly called me and invited me to go down while they were there, so I met Mr. Stratton then, as well as his nephew, Mr. Hollis. And then later I went out and visited..."

But Mildred interrupted. "What was that you said? Stratton?"

"That's right," Anne said. "Mr. Percy Stratton. He lives in State College but on the road to Blue Hill."

"Percy Stratton," Mildred said in a wondering tone. "*He* donated the vase that was stolen? Well, I'll be."

"Mildred, you don't mean that you *know* him, do you?" But even as she asked it, Anne said to herself, *well, why not?* Both Mildred and Mr. Stratton had spent most of their lives in the area, and Mr. Stratton had mentioned that he and his wife had grown up in Blue Hill. They could easily be acquainted.

Would Mildred know something about Mr. Stratton's vase collection? Or have some other piece of information that would throw new light on the theft that would allow Anne to help Wendy?

But Mildred was shaking her head. "I can't really say I know him, but I know *of* him." She paused. "And I know some things about him, thanks to Edie."

"Aunt Edie?" Anne asked in surprise.

"Oh yes," Mildred said. "It was many years ago, but Edie and Percy Stratton had quite a set-to."

"So Aunt Edie knew him?" Anne asked, feeling more and more confused.

Mildred shook her head. "Not a set-to in person," she said. "In the newspaper."

Chapter Twenty-One

Patrick Henry," said Anne in a low voice, understanding dawning at last. She looked thoughtfully at Mildred for a moment. "This set-to that he had with Aunt Edie, did it have to do with her book? The one about the nesting dolls?"

Mildred's face brightened. "Yes, that's it. He'd written some terrible, nasty things to the paper about her book. Practically accused her of being a communist. And then Edie wrote a reply, and he wrote an even nastier letter. They went on like that for a while, but Edie was so smart and so articulate that she eventually managed to get him to see the error of his ways. In the end, he wrote her an apology."

Anne's face clouded with confusion. "But Mildred, his letters to the newspaper were printed under a pseudonym. How did Aunt Edie know who he was?"

Mildred looked thoughtful. "I'd forgotten that. But you're right, at first she didn't know. She just responded to the letters as they appeared." Mildred paused as if thinking back. "It came out in the end. I don't recall how, but eventually Edie did learn who he was, and quite a bit about him too." She shook her head. "He'd had a lot of trouble in his life, poor man. Edie felt quite sorry for him when she learned his story."

"How so?" Anne asked quietly.

Mildred pursed her lips. "Well, I guess the first thing to say is that he just wasn't a very nice man. Quick to anger, quick to take offense. And that sort's always going to have lots of misery anyway. But around the time that Edie had that set-to with him, he had a couple of worse things happen, back to back. First, his wife had died. Some illness, cancer maybe. And then a year or so later, his only son was killed in Vietnam. Apparently he got more ill-tempered and ornery after that, and he just kept getting worse.

"As I said, your aunt Edie managed to get him to come around and apologize about their business, though I wouldn't say he was gracious about it. But he did it." She shook her head. "I don't know what happened to him after that. To tell you the truth, I'm surprised to hear that he's still alive."

"Yes," said Anne, feeling equally surprised. "Alive and making donations to the library."

* * *

That night, after she'd put the kids to bed, Anne pulled out the clippings of the Patrick Henry letters to read through them again. Before, she had skipped through them at random, but she now carefully arranged them in chronological order so that she could read them in sequence.

As Mildred had said, the first letter from "Patrick Henry" had a nasty tone. Because the nesting dolls were Russian, he claimed, they were necessarily the products of a communist society. Even if they had not first been made under communism, they had been subsequently co-opted and should not be of interest to "patriotic Americans."

What bothered Anne even more than the blinded jingoism was the condescending and dismissive attitude toward "lady writers." The international and political realms were the province of men, the letter said, and right-thinking American women should be focusing on traditional American crafts such as quilting. When they dabbled in areas beyond their expertise, they risked allowing their natural sentimentality to undermine the firm resolve and vigilance required in the face of the worldwide communist threat.

Anne was interested to see that in her first response, Aunt Edie did not address the letter's blatant sexism at all. Instead, she focused on the error of equating all aspects of a nation's history and culture with the country's current political regime. There was nothing inherently Russian about communism, Aunt Edie pointed out. Other countries, some very different from Russia, were also communist. And not all Russians were communists, nor were all aspects of Russian culture.

Aunt Edie went out of her way, Anne noted, to agree with Patrick Henry that Soviet-style communism represented a threat and a challenge to Western democracies. But she insisted that it did not necessarily follow that everything associated with Russia was automatically part of that threat. The novels of Tolstoy and Dostoevsky, the music of Tchaikovsky and Stravinsky, or the films of Eisenstein belonged to the world and not just to the Soviets. Likewise, a traditional craft such as the nesting dolls could be appreciated by people the world over without subscribing to the political regime then in power in Russia.

The day might come, Aunt Edie said, when Russia could be persuaded to abandon communism, but these other products of the Russian imagination would live on. Reading these lines, Anne was impressed by her aunt's keen intuition.

Despite her aunt's respect and understanding, the reply from Patrick Henry was even more malicious, as Mildred had recalled. He accused Edie of deliberately trying to promote sympathy for "America's enemies" and of offering "aid and comfort to freedom's foes." The letter was not only nastier but also more incoherent, and Anne was surprised the newspaper had been willing to run it. She doubted very much that Grace Hawkins would have allowed such a letter to appear.

Nevertheless, Aunt Edie responded with even greater grace and forbearance than she had shown before. She patiently restated her argument and she respectfully refuted the charge that her patriotism was in any way lacking. She reminded Patrick Henry that in a free society, disagreement was not treason and that, indeed, insisting that everyone think and believe the same thing was one of the practices that made Soviet communism so antithetical to American values.

In a free society, Aunt Edie said, we have not only the right but the *responsibility* to try to understand the cultures of other nations, especially those so different from our own.

Something in Aunt Edie's letter must have hit home, Anne thought, because after that, the tone of the subsequent Patrick Henry letters began to change, becoming less hysterical and more thoughtful and engaged. The exchange evolved into a discussion of the rights and responsibilities of citizens living in a free society, and it attracted letters from other correspondents. Edie Summers and Patrick Henry—or Percy Stratton—would never agree on every issue, but they did find some common ground, and eventually, as Mildred had said, Patrick Henry expressed regret for the tone of his first couple of letters, even if he never completely renounced the ideas they expressed.

As she set the last clipping aside, Anne wondered at what point in the exchange Aunt Edie had learned Patrick Henry's true identity. There was no change in the tone of her letters that might suggest new knowledge about her antagonist. She had been respectful and understanding throughout, going out of her way to consider and appreciate the arguments on the other side, even while she remained firm in her own convictions.

For a moment, it was almost as if Anne felt her aunt's presence near her, guiding her. Anne thought about her own situation involving letters to the newspaper and the trouble she had been having in writing an appropriate response. She realized she had not been giving due consideration to the feelings and concerns of her critics. In all her drafts to date, her response had focused on expressing her own opinions and defending her actions.

But Aunt Edie's example showed that she first needed to find the common ground on which she and her critics could meet and communicate. And that common ground was surely the concern for the well-being of children that was a priority of both parents and librarians.

Setting aside the clippings from Aunt Edie's exchanges with Percy Stratton, Anne pulled out a blank pad of paper and began to draft a fresh response of her own.

* * *

"Anne?" Wendy's voice on Saturday morning sounded exhausted. "We're home."

"How was Maine?" Anne asked eagerly. "Did you have a good time? Did the kids? I can't wait to hear all about it."

"I think," said Wendy slowly, "that it will turn out that we had a good time." She paused, as if considering the options. "Yes, I think it's fairly likely that we'll decide we had a good time."

"I see," said Anne. "And just what is preventing you from deciding that right now?"

"Lack of sleep," Wendy replied. "Someday soon, when I have had a serious amount of sleep, I am confident that I will look back on the trip and conclude that we had a good time." The sound of a stifled yawn came down the line. "In fact, I'm rather looking forward to reaching that conclusion. You know, someday. First, sleep. Then perhaps I'd better check and make sure that we returned with the same number of children that we started out with. If we've lost some along the way, I suppose that could put a damper on things. But I won't know until I've had some sleep."

"Perhaps you'll find that you've returned with more kids than you set out with," Anne suggested, smiling.

"As long as they don't try to interfere with my sleep," Wendy replied.

"Listen, I'm glad you called," Anne said with feigned nonchalance. "Betty called in sick this morning. Since you're home now, maybe you could come in for a couple of hours?"

Wendy hesitated for only a fraction of a second before saying, "That's what I like about you, Anne. Your sense of humor. That keen wit. You're a regular card, you are."

Anne laughed. "Seriously, though, if you need to rest and recover, don't worry about coming in next week."

"But it's summer! You'll be swamped!"

"I can manage. I mean," Anne added quickly, worried that Wendy might get the wrong message, "it's up to you, of course. You just shouldn't feel obligated. You have enough on your mind already." She regretted adding that last part as soon as it was out of her mouth, but she couldn't recall it.

Wendy's voice lost its playfulness but still sounded very tired. "We'll see. Thanks for the offer. I may take you up on it. Because seriously, I gotta get some sleep."

Anne chastised herself as she hung up the phone. When she'd called, Wendy had sounded more like her old self than she had since the trouble about being a "suspect" had begun. But Anne, with her clumsy remark at the end, had brought it all back into Wendy's mind, negating the distraction and distance that the family vacation to Maine had provided.

She hadn't even shared the discovery about the mysterious collector, Ambrose Carron, or his possible connection with Angie Staub.

Though on second thought, perhaps Anne should wait to share that news until she'd heard back from Michael Banks. After all, if that proved to be nothing, then she might end up raising Wendy's hopes only to dash them again.

She hadn't told Wendy about her visit to Percy Stratton, either. Nor had Wendy asked, even though Anne had told her about the planned visit just before Wendy left on vacation. She tried to weigh the significance of that. Was Wendy trying to put all the "suspect" business behind her? Was she finally coming around to Anne's opinion that it would all sort itself out in the end? Or was she so stressed out about it that she couldn't even face hearing about Anne's trip to visit Mr. Stratton?

Or maybe, Anne, thought ruefully, Wendy was just tired after a long trip. Like she'd said.

As she had been so often in the past few days, Anne was back to feeling desperate to help her friend and absolutely stymied about how to do so. Once again, she began to review her mental list of people who might be able to throw light on the case. Miles Bridges and Angie Staub she had just seen. Who else was there?

She recalled her visit to the police station the day before, when she'd gone to share her discovery about Carron. Would Michael Banks have had a chance to pursue that lead yet? Would it be too pushy to call him up and ask?

Why had Miles Bridges been so quick to defend Angie Staub? Was it merely professional loyalty? Because he was the one who had brought her into the auction? Or did he have some guilty knowledge about what the two of them had been up to?

Anne realized she hadn't given much consideration to Miles as a suspect. Perhaps she should do so.

She stared at the phone, but she felt it really was too soon to call Michael and ask for another update. Surely he had given Miles due consideration as a suspect, even if Anne hadn't. Although, now that she thought about it, the two of them had seemed awfully relaxed and friendly when she'd come upon them the day before. *What had they been discussing? Oh yes, extra security for the auction.*

Security.

That was the piece that had been nagging at the back of Anne's mind: Theo the Security Guard. The guy who ought to have been able to clear Wendy.

Anne had asked Michael about him, but she couldn't recall that he'd given her much of an answer. Had he promised to talk to him again? That was what Anne had wanted him to do, but she didn't think he had actually promised to do so.

Could Anne do so?

She didn't know his last name. Nor did Wendy. Could she just go down to the museum and ask for him? She thought she recalled Wendy saying that he worked the weekend shift.

That afternoon, she asked Ben and Liddie if they'd like to make another trip to the museum and received the enthusiastic agreement that she'd been counting on.

As soon as they walked in, Anne began keeping a sharp eye out for the security guards on duty, and especially for their nametags. There appeared to be two, and it was immediately obvious that Doreen, positioned by the door, was not her man.

Anne allowed Ben and Liddie to wander at will about the museum while she drifted among the exhibits, trying to look casual. She had already half-convinced herself that the second guard must be the elusive Theo.

Unfortunately, "elusive" was turning out to be more than apt. With Doreen stationed at the entrance, this guy's job appeared to be circulating throughout the rest of the museum. Every time that Anne, in her feigned casualness, managed to move in his direction, he would purposefully stride off to some other part of the museum.

She couldn't get close enough to read his nametag, though from a distance, the name engraved on it appeared rather long. Theodore, perhaps?

She soon began to feel like she was stalking him, but he seemed oblivious to her movements. Between trying to keep one eye on her quarry and one eye on her kids, Anne was paying almost no attention to the displays that she was passing.

She stopped before a large display case in order to collect herself. Clearly a more direct approach was called for here, rather than this sneaking about.

She took a deep breath, turned, and walked directly toward Theo the Security Guard, thinking that the best approach would be simply to explain that she wanted to help her friend.

She came to an abrupt halt about two feet away, staring at the guard's chest.

The nametag said, *Archibald*.

After she had stared for a few moments, she realized the guard was looking at her with a puzzled, expectant expression. "Can I help you, ma'am?"

Blushing furiously, Anne stammered, "I'm sorry. I…I thought you were someone else. Is Theo here?"

The guard shook his head and replied, "Nope." He had a wary look in his eyes.

"Do you know when he'll be on duty next?" Anne asked.

"Nope," the guard replied tersely.

Anne could see she wasn't going to get anywhere with this obviously suspicious guard. A few minutes later, she managed to collect her children and flee the museum.

Chapter Twenty-Two

Anne spent the rest of the evening pondering Theo the MIA Security Guard, and by midmorning on Monday, despite the library's constant stream of summer traffic, she put in a call to Michael Banks.

"He's gone," she said, as soon as she had Michael on the phone.

"Who's gone, Anne?" he asked after a resigned sigh.

"Sorry. Theo the Security Guard. The guy who was there when Wendy went back for her phone. The one who can confirm her story. Or, well, almost confirm it. And now he's gone. Doesn't that strike you as suspicious?"

Sounding genuinely curious, Michael asked, "How do you know he's gone?"

"Because I went to the museum on Saturday and he wasn't there. Archibald was there instead. Saturday is Theo's night because it was Saturday when Wendy left her phone after the meeting. But when I went *this* Saturday, he wasn't there."

"And just why were you looking for Theo at the museum, Anne?" She was becoming familiar with this note of annoyance in his voice.

"Oh well, I thought I would just talk to him myself about that night. Just to hear the firsthand account."

"I told you that we questioned Theo."

"I know, but you didn't go back and do it again, and I just thought maybe I would. And it looks now like it's a good thing I did, because he seems to have fled."

"Fled? Anne, are you suggesting that Theo may have had something to do with the theft?"

"Don't you see? That's why he's trying to cast suspicion on Wendy. So it won't fall on him. And now it's given him a chance to make his getaway."

There was an odd sound on the other end of the line that Anne finally identified as suppressed chuckling. Her suspicions about Theo, so strong a moment before, began to crumble.

After a moment, Michael said, "So you went to the museum on Saturday and you didn't see Theo."

"That's right," Anne replied cautiously.

"And you went while the museum was open?" Anne began to suspect where this was going. "Because the guards work in shifts, and Theo is on the night shift. He doesn't go on duty until the museum is closed for the day. You see?"

Chagrined, Anne said, "Yes, I see." But her own embarrassment was minor compared to the dashing of her fresh hopes for clearing Wendy.

"We're keeping tabs on Theo," Michael said. "Not that I really suspect him, but I'm pretty sure he hasn't skipped town."

Feeling contrite, Anne said, "I'm sorry, Michael."

"That's okay. Listen, the timing of your call is good, because I was going to ask you to come down to the station again this afternoon anyway. Percy Stratton's nephew has been able to come to town and the two of them are coming in for an update. Since you and Stratton are the apparent victims here, I can update you all at the same time."

* * *

After so many visits recently, Anne was becoming quite familiar with the Blue Hill Police Station. She stepped through the door, waved to the receptionist, and strode toward the chairs and the spindly plant, where Percy Stratton and Ronald Hollis sat.

From the corner of her eye, she noticed the receptionist pick up the receiver on her phone and press a single button.

"Mr. Stratton. Mr. Hollis. It's a pleasure to see you both again."

She watched Mr. Stratton closely but discreetly, trying to gauge today's level of mental engagement. His behavior seemed more like when she had visited his house than when he had first visited the police station. Mr. Hollis was still something of an enigma to her, and neither man returned her greeting with much enthusiasm.

"So I guess Michael has an update for us," she said. "I mean, Officer Banks."

This observation received a curt nod from Mr. Hollis, and no response at all from his uncle.

"I enjoyed visiting you at your home last week, Mr. Stratton," she tried.

This earned a sharp glance from Mr. Hollis, but Mr. Stratton looked pleased. "That's right, that's right," he said, as if he'd forgotten but now remembered. "That was some fine banana bread you brought. I finished it up!"

Anne smiled. "I'm glad you liked it."

The door to the rest of the station opened and Michael Banks stepped through. He nodded to all of them and thanked them for coming. "With the auction coming up on Saturday, I wanted to give you all a sense of where we stand."

With that, he ushered them through to the same conference room in which they had met before. The three men allowed Anne to enter first, and she found the table covered with a mess of items. After a moment, she realized it was all evidence that pertained to the case. She saw photographs of the stolen vase and the replacement vase strewn across the table, as well as photographs of the display cabinet, the storerooms at the museum, and other shots. At the far end of the conference table, the second vase sat in a box on a cushion of Styrofoam peanuts. It was still in a large, clear plastic bag, but it was clearly the vase.

Anne stepped around to the far side of the table and turned so that she was facing the other three as they entered. She saw them all quickly survey the mass of pictures and items on the table, as she had done, as they each sought chairs at the near end of the table, which was not so cluttered. She heard Michael utter an exclamation of dismay when he saw the state of the table.

Just as he laid his hand on the back of a chair, Percy Stratton gave a start and stared hard at the vase at the far end of the table. A smile spread across his features. "You've found it!" he exclaimed. "What do you know, I hadn't expected this."

He turned a delighted expression on Michael Banks, who was trying to push the mess farther down the table. At Mr. Stratton's remark, Michael looked up, puzzled.

"No, Uncle, no," Mr. Hollis said sharply. "That's not the vase you donated. That's the one that was left in its place."

Anne was surprised to see Mr. Hollis watching his uncle with great concern. Perhaps Mr. Stratton's mental acuity today was worse than she had thought.

Mr. Stratton seemed taken aback by his nephew's vehemence and his smile quickly faded.

"At least," Mr. Hollis continued, though not quite so urgently, "I assume that's what it is. Isn't it, Officer Banks?"

Michael looked from Hollis to the vase at the far end of the table. "Yes, that's right. I'm sorry, Mr. Stratton, I didn't mean to... Actually, this was all supposed to be cleared out of here." He continued pushing things to the far end of the table. When he was satisfied, he looked up and said, "Your nephew is correct, Mr. Stratton. That vase is the one that was left behind as a decoy when your vase was stolen."

Whatever else was going on, Anne felt a little twinge of satisfaction when Michael said "your" vase to Percy Stratton.

"Thank you all again for coming in," Michael began. As Anne looked around the table, it seemed to her that Mr. Stratton's face still wore a troubled expression and he kept glancing at the vase, while his nephew watched him with concern. She wondered if there was any danger of Mr. Stratton having some sort of episode right there in the conference room.

After a distracted moment, Hollis turned to Michael and replied, "We appreciate your efforts at keeping us informed, Officer Banks."

Michael nodded. "The first thing I want to do is update you on a line of inquiry that Anne helped uncover." He explained about Angie Staub and her connection to the collector Ambrose Carron.

"You said that Angie brought someone by your house to look at the vases, Mr. Stratton," Anne said, interrupting Michael in her eagerness. "I think that's the man she brought."

Michael reached into the clutter on the tabletop, pulled out an enlargement of the photo of Carron, and slid it across to Mr. Stratton. "Is this the man that Angie Staub brought to your house, sir?"

Mr. Stratton, who had been nodding vigorously while people spoke, stopped suddenly and his face grew troubled. He leaned over the photograph on the table, then picked it up and held it close to his eyes. Finally, he pushed the picture away from him and muttered, "Could be, could be." His nephew gently patted his forearm a couple of times.

Michael looked closely at Mr. Stratton for a moment and then said, "Well, it's a moot point. We've tracked down Carron and talked to him, and we've talked to Angie Staub. The two of them had cooked up a scheme to buy the vase at the auction and then resell it. They seemed to think they could get it for less than its real value."

"But why would they think that?" Anne asked. "It was well known that the vase is valuable. That story from the *Gazette* got picked up by other papers all around the state. Why did they think they could count on getting a deal? Because this is a small community auction?"

Ronald Hollis cleared his throat. "How much do they think the vase is worth? Did they say?"

"My understanding is that the vase was appraised at ten thousand dollars," Michael said, "and that Mr. Bridges and Ms. Staub confirmed that. But I think, as Anne suggests, they thought they could get it for much less because this is a small auction in a small town. And Ms. Staub, as the person who might have alerted other interested buyers, chose to share that information with only one collector, on the condition that they immediately resell and split the profits."

"And would that actually be illegal?" Anne asked.

"Mr. Bridges assures me that such collusion would certainly be unethical, particularly in these circumstances, but it's not actually illegal. I've informed him of what we've learned, and I understand that he has stopped working with Ms. Staub."

Percy Stratton resumed his vigorous nodding.

"Okay," Anne said slowly, "but how did they get from sweetheart deal to actually stealing the vase? Did word about its value circulate too widely? Or were they unable to put together the funds for the auction purchase? Carron expressed interest in buying it preemptively, but he didn't follow up on that. So what changed their plans?"

"That's the thing," said Michael slowly. "Whatever plans they cooked up, they were never carried out. Both Staub and Carron have airtight alibis as far as the theft is concerned. Neither one of them could possibly have done it."

The entire group looked grim, and Anne felt a stab of disappointment. She'd had such hopes that this development would help resolve the mystery.

After a moment, Mr. Hollis asked, "So Ms. Staub is no longer in the picture?"

Michael nodded.

"Well, then, we certainly appreciate your efforts, Officer Banks," Mr. Hollis said in the tone of someone winding up the conversation.

But Michael said, "There is one other piece of information that I wanted to share."

Mr. Hollis settled down again and looked attentive.

"Again," Michael continued in an apologetic tone, "this is something that Anne may have heard already from Miles Bridges, but I wanted to make sure the two of you were aware of it as well. It concerns that vase there." Their heads all swiveled toward the other end of the table. "Mr. Bridges tells me that the replacement vase is almost equal in value to the one that was stolen."

Neither Mr. Stratton nor Mr. Hollis seemed to react to this news. Mr. Stratton stared off into space, dark clouds on his brow. Mr. Hollis looked a little bored until he became aware of Anne's eyes upon him. Then he suddenly sat up straight and assumed a look of surprise.

"That seems very odd, doesn't it, officer? To steal one vase but leave behind another that's worth just as much? That can't happen very often, does it?"

"No, Mr. Hollis," Michael replied. "It's very odd. I've never seen or heard of anything like it. And it has certainly complicated the investigation, as it's hard to imagine what the thief's motive might be. But the reason I bring it up is because eventually there's going to be a question as to who the rightful owner of this second vase is." He looked carefully at each of them.

"Oh well," said Mr. Hollis nervously, "clearly that would be the library."

Anne's eyebrows shot up, since this was not at all clear to her.

Michael asked, "You think so?"

"Of course," said Mr. Hollis. "If you take the idea that this vase was left behind as a kind of…replacement for the one that was stolen, something to make good the damage, then it ought to be auctioned off in place of the other one, it seems to me, and the proceeds should still go to the library. That way, the library would still receive the contribution that my uncle wanted to make." He turned toward the old man and said, "Don't you think so, Uncle Percy?"

But Mr. Stratton was scowling down at the table and did not reply.

"Something to 'make good the damage,' you say?" Michael said thoughtfully. "Well, it's a point of view, for sure, though I've never seen or heard of such an altruistic criminal in the past. I don't think that was the thief's purpose in leaving it behind, however."

"Well then, what do you think his purpose was?" Mr. Hollis demanded.

"That's the problem," Michael admitted. "I don't have a better explanation." He rubbed his hand across his jaw. "I suspect that the thief may have been unaware of the second vase's value. Because if he knew about it, why go to the trouble of stealing the first one? He apparently already had a valuable Chinese vase in his possession. But suppose he didn't know it. Perhaps he had already stolen it from someone else, unaware of its value. But he knew the value of the vase in the auction, because the story was all over town. So if he didn't know the second vase's value, he might have decided to leave it behind in an effort to hide his theft for as long as possible." Michael shrugged. "It's still pretty farfetched, but it would explain the odd circumstance of the second vase's value."

To Anne's surprise, Mr. Hollis had a discontented look on his face. "I still think the library ought to benefit from it," he said.

But when he glanced up and saw Anne looking at him, he quickly looked away again.

Chapter Twenty-Three

As Anne had anticipated, summertime was extremely busy for the library. A steady stream of students came by her desk, bearing the summer reading lists their teachers had distributed. Some of the teachers had shared their lists with Anne in advance, so she had been able to collect the books, but other lists she had not seen before. Once she had copies of the new lists, she was able to begin pulling those books from the shelves as well.

Anne put the books onto a cart by the checkout desk for easy access. The students who showed up early to collect their summer reading quickly grabbed whichever book was the shortest. Students arriving later gazed at the remaining selection with dismay. Some even asked if there were shorter books available, and when Anne explained that those had already been checked out, they were invariably shocked to discover that they'd been beaten to the punch. Perhaps the other books would be returned by the time they were ready for the next one, she suggested, knowing that each student was required to read three selections from the list over the course of the summer.

A few students had criteria other than length in mind, and these quizzed Anne on the nature, style, and content of each book on the list. When they'd set their hearts on a specific book that had already been checked out, Anne would promise to hold the library's copy when it was returned. Many of these students left with their three selections for the summer all made, and a few even checked out additional books not on the list.

Next summer, Anne thought, she would try to coordinate with the teachers and perhaps establish a summer reading club that could be integrated with the school's requirements.

On Wednesday, Anne was able to snatch her usual few minutes to read the new edition of the *Blue Hill Gazette*. This was the issue in which "the librarian responds to her critics," as Anne had dubbed it, and she was eager to see how her letter looked on the page.

The front page was devoted to the appraisal fair and auction to be held that weekend. Anne was amused to note that with the event so close, the theft of the vase once again rated a small, boxed feature on the front page even though there was nothing new to report.

She quickly turned to the opinion pages to see what she would find.

The first thing she did was read her own letter. She tried to do so as objectively as possible, while keeping in mind the example of Aunt Edie's responses to Patrick Henry. She finished with a small smile of satisfaction on her lips. She felt she had succeeded in adopting Aunt Edie's approach—she had acknowledged the concerns of those who had complained and had tried to establish common ground with them on the question of when and how one should try to shield children. She had lightly invoked her training and experience in this area as a librarian, and she had firmly stated her position on the appropriateness of the materials.

It might not convince or silence her critics, but she felt that she had explained her position well enough that she wouldn't need to do so again. For readers who remained unconvinced, they would simply have to agree to disagree.

Anne turned her attention to the other letters. There were three others about the display and the discussion around it. The writers were all unfamiliar to her, but she couldn't help feeling gratified that two had written in her defense and only one was echoing the earlier criticism. The one critic seemed to feel that children should always be shielded from anything upsetting or unpleasant, without exception, while those in Anne's defense criticized this view as a failure of adults' responsibility to educate children and prepare them for life in the real world.

What surprised Anne the most, however, was that Grace Hawkins had written an editorial related to the issue as well. She didn't address the question of what was appropriate or not for children, but rather the importance of knowing and understanding history, both the good and the bad. To illustrate her editorial, Grace had run a photograph of her own from the Jim Crow era, showing separate drinking fountains with signs for "whites" and "coloreds."

In a separate box, Grace had added a note celebrating the fact that Anne's column about books and the library would be appearing on a monthly basis.

Smiling, Anne thought she'd better get busy on the next one.

* * *

Despite the hectic week at the library, Anne's mind had been constantly reverting to her visit to the police station at the beginning of the week.

Friday arrived, the eve of the Antique Appraisal Fair and Auction, and she was still unable to stop thinking about it. She decided that a fresh perspective was in order, and since things in the library had calmed by Friday afternoon, she set out to consult a trusted advisor.

She found Reverend Tom in his office at the church, at work on his sermon for Sunday. He welcomed the chance to take a break, he assured her, and waved her to a chair with a smile.

As he resumed his own seat, he said, "I'm going to take a wild guess here that you are still concerned about Wendy." He cocked an eyebrow.

"Yes," said Anne. "But it's not just her. It's this whole situation."

Reverend Tom nodded. "I gather the police haven't made much progress."

"We thought we had a lead for a while," Anne said, "but the police called us in on Monday to tell us it didn't pan out."

"We?" Reverend Tom asked with a frown. "Was Wendy with you?"

"Oh no. Sorry. It was Mr. Stratton, the man who donated the vase, Ronald Hollis, who is his nephew, and me. I haven't seen Wendy since the Pyles got back from their trip. I've just talked with her on the phone a couple of times. And that feels weird right there."

"She hasn't been working at the library?"

"I gave her the week off, thinking that she might need time to recover from the vacation. I'm hoping we'll get back to our usual schedule next week. But now I'm worried she's just spent this entire week holed up in her house. That can't be good!"

Tom said quietly, "Well, I know for a fact that she's gotten out some."

He said no more, but Anne suspected that this was a way of telling her that Wendy had been in to see him, presumably to talk about her troubles. Anne was relieved to hear this, though she understood that she could not press for details.

Reverend Tom said, "So you've found out who the mysterious donor is." He made it a statement rather than a question.

"Yes. A man named Percy Stratton. He lives in State College, on the road to Blue Hill. He's quite elderly and is developing dementia."

"Hence the nephew you mentioned?"

Anne nodded.

"Does the dementia have anything to do with why he chose to make the donation to the library?"

"No, he seems to be quite clear about that. And the nephew as well. No, I think there's something else going on there."

Reverend Tom spread his hands to invite her to continue.

Anne told him about the exchange of letters in the newspaper between Aunt Edie and "Patrick Henry" and the fact that the anonymous Henry was, in fact, Percy Stratton. "Whenever I see him, he keeps telling me what a remarkable person Aunt Edie was," she concluded.

"Well, that's true enough," Reverend Tom said.

"Yes, but as far as I can tell, he never actually met her. The only contact that they ever had was through this exchange of letters."

Reverend Tom nodded. "And you say this occurred at a period in his life when he had suffered great loss?"

"First his wife, then his son," Anne said, nodding. "And Aunt Edie's letters to him are full of compassion and understanding, even, as far as I can tell, before she knew the details of his circumstances or even who he was. I think they made a difference at a difficult time and that he remembers them to this day. He mentioned that he had only recently heard of Aunt Edie's passing and of the creation of the library. I suspect he had intended to do something in her honor for a while, and then learned about the library."

"It's a great blessing, to be able to pay our debts," Reverend Tom observed, "even after years have elapsed. But are you sure the nephew is on board with all this? People can get awfully funny if they think an inheritance is slipping away. And even with the purest of motives, people can get protective of elderly relatives who develop dementia. Are you sure there's no chance for misunderstanding there?"

"I don't think so," Anne said. "Mr. Hollis was the one insisting that the library should have the second vase."

"Second vase...," Reverend Tom said thoughtfully. "That's right, I'd forgotten. But why would the library *want* the second vase?"

"Because it's not exactly a phony, as everyone assumes it is. It's worth almost as much as the first one."

Reverend Tom sat bolt upright and stared at Anne. "That's astonishing! Somebody stole the vase but left behind another that was just as valuable? I had no idea."

"I don't think I'm really supposed to be talking about that," Anne said, not because she was worried about telling Reverend Tom, but just to make sure that he understood it was not common knowledge.

"Of course. But still, that's very surprising." His face grew thoughtful. "I suppose it must suggest a motive for the crime completely different from greed. The thief must have had some deep personal connection to that particular vase, that he should go to the trouble and danger of stealing it and yet leave behind one of equal value."

"I've thought about that," Anne said, "but Mr. Stratton claims that he has owned that vase for decades. So how could somebody else have developed that kind of an attachment to that particular vase, when it's been sitting for all these years on a shelf in his house?" Anne thought for a moment. "Michael Banks thinks that the thief may not have realized that the second vase was also valuable."

"Perhaps," said Reverend Tom in a dissatisfied tone, "but in that case, how did he get his hands on it? You don't just find such things lying by the roadside.""

"We already know he's a thief," Anne said. "Perhaps he stole it from somebody else?"

She could tell from Reverend Tom's face that he still found this explanation unsatisfying, but he reverted to an earlier topic by asking, "And this nephew thinks the library should have the second vase?"

"He made an odd remark about the second vase being a replacement for the first one. I suppose, when you realize that it's worth the same, you might think of it in those terms, though presumably the thief didn't. But yes, Mr. Hollis thought we should go ahead and auction the second vase and have the proceeds go to the library."

"Would that be possible?"

"Michael says no. To begin with, the second vase is still evidence in an ongoing investigation. And the legal owner of the second vase is still unclear. Just because Mr. Stratton and Mr. Hollis think it should belong to the library doesn't mean they can actually make that decision."

Reverend Tom nodded slowly. "So what about this Mr. Stratton? Just how bad is his dementia?"

Anne shrugged. "I'm not sure. I've seen him on three occasions now, and each time he seemed very different. The first time at the police station, he seemed quite out of it, and Miles told me that he was having a bad day. The second time was at his own house. He seemed much sharper that time and also crankier, which I understand is his usual state. Perhaps being in familiar surroundings helped." Anne grew hesitant. "The third time was at the police station again, and at first I thought he seemed very much like I'd seen him in his own home. He seemed alert and aware of what was going on around him. And yet there was an incident later on that suggested maybe he wasn't as present as I'd thought."

"What happened?"

"We walked into the police conference room, and there was all this evidence from the case spread out on the table. And at one end was that second vase. It was inside a plastic bag and in a box, but you could still see it fairly well. When Mr. Stratton looked at it, he thought it was the first vase, his own vase. He thought the police had recovered it."

"Is that so odd?" Reverend Tom asked. "I thought they looked similar."

Anne nodded. "They do. But the first vase was his own property, and yet he was so sure that he recognized this one. And then when Mr. Hollis corrected him, he seemed to grow very confused. That's what makes me think that the dementia may have been worse that day than I'd originally thought."

Anne stared at the top of Reverend Tom's desk as she thought back to her various encounters with Mr. Stratton. "And as far as that goes," she added, "there was a similar moment when he was in his home. He was looking at the shelves where the rest of his collection was on display, and he had a moment of confusion then too. He was looking for the vase that had been his wife's favorite, and he couldn't…he couldn't…"

Anne's voice trailed off. Reverend Tom sat and watched her.

Finally Anne looked up, feeling both troubled and intrigued. "Reverend," she said, "I think I need to go talk with Michael Banks again. Do you think you could come with me?"

Chapter Twenty-Four

The day of the Antique Appraisal Fair and Auction was cloudless but not too hot, perfect weather for the Railroad Days celebrations.

Before Anne had left Reverend Tom's office on Friday, he had encouraged her to reach out to Wendy, so Anne called her early Saturday morning to arrange a place and time to meet at the fair. Anne was afraid Wendy wouldn't want to attend the event, but she'd forgotten that there was a stronger force at work than pride or embarrassment—maternal obligation. Wendy needed to get her daughter Hannah to the fair early because she was participating in Hal McCollum's oral history project.

Anne had a similar obligation because Ben had decided to help out with the oral histories as well, so they all agreed to meet at the tents that had been set up for recording the histories.

The appraisal fair was being held in the spacious parking lot of the Railroad Museum, which had been built to accommodate rail passengers rather than museum-goers. Automobiles had been banished and numerous tents, large and small, had been set up around the lot. Those devoted to the appraisals had been grouped according to the kinds of items to be evaluated: furniture, fine art, ceramics, toys, and many other categories. There were also food tents, historical exhibits, some old-fashioned games for the kids, and the tents in which the oral histories were being collected.

There were some attractions inside the museum as well, but the weather was so fine that almost everything could be held outside.

Anne, Ben, and Liddie met up with Wendy and Hannah, as arranged, and Wendy took charge of delivering Ben and Hannah to Hal McCollum.

When she returned, she looked a little sheepish. "I'm sorry I didn't come by the library this week."

Anne gave the most reassuring smile she could. "I'm sure you had an awful lot to catch up on after your trip. "You'll be back to your usual schedule next week?"

Wendy grinned. "You bet." She looked down at Liddie, who stood next to a wheeled cart whose basket was almost as tall as she was. It was full of packages. "What've you got there, Liddie? Are those the nesting dolls?"

Liddie nodded, an excited smile on her face.

"It hadn't occurred to me that I would need to transport them," Anne said as they began to stroll around the fair. "You think of nesting dolls and you think of something nice and compact, since they can all go inside one another. But I've got so many different sets! I spent half an hour running around last night just looking for this cart."

"It looks handy," Wendy offered, glancing down at it.

"You see them all over the place in Brooklyn," Anne said. "They're perfect for the city. But here in Blue Hill, I haven't had the same need for it."

Wendy nodded. "Out here in the country, we just throw everything into the trunk of the car," she said with a laugh. "Come on, let's see what people have brought to have appraised."

Anne may have found it a challenge to cart her multiple sets of matryoshka dolls around, but she soon saw that she had it easy compared to what other visitors were putting themselves through. She and Wendy were fascinated with the section devoted to appraising furniture. People were bringing desks, dressers, and other large pieces, wrapped in padded blankets and perched on dollies. Most visitors had brought family members to help, though the fair provided volunteers to assist as well.

Many pieces by the tents had been set up and unwrapped, ready for inspection, while other items were carried back and forth in a surprisingly steady stream. Those waiting their turn to be evaluated were inspected by interested members of the crowd, with their owners standing by, beaming and ready to answer questions to the best of their ability. Anne and Wendy mostly admired the furniture from a safe distance, since Anne didn't want to risk nicking anything with her cart in the jostling crowd.

With the large pieces of furniture, the appraisers had to move from one to the next, but in most of the tents, the appraisers sat behind a table, and a long queue snaked back from each as the items were taken to the experts.

Anne was suddenly struck by a thought. "Where do we even take these dolls, anyway? What category are they? Toys?"

"Let's see," said Wendy, "I think I can remember the categories we came up with." She mulled it over for a moment, then said, "I know there's a crafts tent, which I think is mostly for folk crafts. I'd say we should try there."

But they were in no hurry, so they continued wandering, allowing Liddie to dart away and return as things caught her eye.

As they strolled about, Wendy told Anne all about their trip to Acadia National Park. They would occasionally encounter Ben, who had been sent out into the crowd to hand out fliers and entice visitors to the oral history booths.

"Are you getting good business?" Wendy asked him.

"Pretty good," he replied, "but Mr. McCollum wants to get as many as possible, so he says I should keep reeling them in. He's also got some people walking around and doing 'on-the-spot' histories. They have these neat little recorders."

"Perhaps you should go do one, Wendy," Anne suggested, and Ben looked up hopefully.

"Hey, I'm not the one who was born and raised in Blue Hill," she objected.

"No, but I was away for so long," Anne said, "whereas you know practically everybody who lives here now."

After a moment, Wendy said, "Well, you know, perhaps I will do one later on." She looked at Ben. "Not right now, though."

Since Wendy was not going to allow herself to be dragged to the microphone that very minute, Ben set off once again with his fliers.

"I should talk with Hal about making these recordings available through the library, don't you think?"

Wendy agreed that this was a good idea.

"It's too bad no one ever did an oral history with Aunt Edie," Anne continued wistfully.

"Oh, she'd have been a perfect candidate," Wendy agreed. "And speaking of candidates, you know who else would be perfect?"

They looked at one another and said, "Mildred Farley."

"If we see her, we'll have to drag her over there," Wendy said with a laugh.

Eventually, they came across the tent devoted to crafts.

It had a much smaller crowd than the ceramics or jewelry tents, which made for a more relaxed atmosphere. They approached the volunteer who was coordinating the section and asked about nesting dolls. There were only two appraisers in this tent and Anne worried that neither one might have the right expertise. But the face of the second appraiser lit up at the mention of nesting dolls, and they were soon ushered to his table.

The appraiser, Mr. Stokes, insisted on bringing out each and every set and then opening each one right down to the smallest member, exclaiming all the while as he did so. Wendy was gratified to have her theory confirmed that at least some of the sets were quite old. She began nudging Anne, convinced that the sets would collectively be worth a considerable amount.

Anne was most surprised when Mr. Stokes reserved his most careful examination for the set that Anne considered to be in the poorest condition. It was clearly old and depicted its figures in traditional peasant costumes. Anne wondered if this was desirable among collectors. But this particular set was also rather battered and beat up. Anne didn't know what to think when Mr. Stokes pulled out a magnifying glass and began carefully examining every flaw and chip in the surfaces. For some reason, he seemed excited by them.

After a moment, she tried, "I guess those marks will affect the value?"

"Yes, yes. Some," he replied with a distracted air, "but that's not..." He moved his glass very quickly from one figure to the next. When he looked up, his eyes were bright. "Excuse me just a moment, will you?"

He turned away and opened up a trunk on the ground behind him. Anne couldn't see what it contained, but he rummaged around inside for a bit, and when he turned back, she was astonished to see that he was holding a copy of Aunt Edie's book on nesting dolls. She exchanged a glance with Wendy but didn't say anything because he was already rapidly flipping through the pages.

At last, he found what he wanted and held the book open before her eyes. "You have this set," he said excitedly, jabbing his finger at a photograph in the book. "Not a set like this, but *this* set."

Anne had not noticed that this set was one of the ones that appeared in the book, but it made sense that some of the photographs would be from Aunt Edie's personal collection.

Stokes was highly excited. "See, see!" he exclaimed, setting the book down and then pointing to various distinguishing marks on dolls in the picture and the dolls on the table before him. After he'd pointed out several, he shook his head in amazement and said again, "It's this very set."

Anne smiled. "Well, Mr. Stokes, as it happens, there's a very good reason for that."

* * *

"But it's the very set," Wendy said indignantly. "And some of the others may be too."

"Yes, I realize that," Anne said, laughing. "And it was very exciting for Mr. Stokes, because he knows the book. But you heard him, it's not going to be that significant to collectors. For them it will be a point of interest, a curiosity, nothing more. He was very definite that it would not increase the value."

Based on her own hopes and on Mr. Stokes's extraordinary reaction, Wendy had become convinced that the collection of matroyshka dolls would prove very valuable. The final estimate of about two thousand dollars had come as a distinct letdown.

Anne, on the other hand, was delighted to have found such a fan of her aunt's book. Mr. Stokes had asked Anne many questions about Edie and had even asked her to autograph his copy of her book.

"I thought it was the person receiving the appraisal who was supposed to have the delightful surprise," Wendy muttered discontentedly, "not the appraiser."

Chapter Twenty-Five

The weather held fine all day, but by evening, clouds began to roll in, and the air grew humid. It was a good thing that they had decided to hold the auction in the fellowship hall at Blue Hill Community Church, Anne thought, and had not tried to hold it outside. The crowd filled the hall to capacity, which made the air feel closer still. But it was the excitement about the event that charged the atmosphere, and the close conditions merely added to the anticipation.

When Hal McCollum strode up the center aisle, the crowd erupted in cheers and applause. In her mind, Anne could hear Wendy saying, *"Auction fever, baby."*

She sat at the very back of the hall with Ben and Liddie, and with Alex Ochs and his nephew, Ryan. Wendy and her family had taken seats farther up.

Hal, wearing a wide grin, waved the crowd to silence. He welcomed everyone and asked how they had enjoyed the appraisal fair, which got the crowd going again. Anne smiled. She had never thought of Hal as a showman. He reminded them that the Community Benefit Auction was the concluding event of the Railroad Days festival, and he wanted to take the opportunity to thank the people who had made it possible. At this, Anne tensed, but when Hal named the members of the steering committee, Wendy was among them. Anne let her shoulders relax.

Hal introduced Miles Bridges, who stepped before the crowd and explained how the auction would work. He had just begun to introduce the first item, a lovely set of china, when Anne felt a tap on her shoulder and turned to see Reverend Tom behind her. She nodded to Alex, who had previously agreed to watch Ben and Liddie when Anne stepped away.

She stood and followed Reverend Tom out. "They're here?"

Reverend Tom nodded as he led her out the door. They walked around to the side parking lot, where they found Percy Stratton and Ronald Hollis emerging from a car.

"Mr. Stratton, I'm so glad you decided to come," Anne said. She turned to his nephew and added, "Thank you for bringing him, Mr. Hollis."

Percy Stratton muttered something about a foolish waste of time, but he seemed otherwise willing to be there. Anne introduced them to Reverend Tom, who led them toward the entrance at the rear of the main building.

When they entered, however, Reverend Tom did not turn toward the fellowship hall but instead in the direction of his own office, saying, "I wonder if we might first have a word, gentlemen?"

Inside his office, Michael Banks waited for them.

Reverend Tom guided Mr. Stratton and Mr. Hollis to the two chairs, leaving Anne and Michael to stand while he stepped around the desk and sat in his usual place.

"Now then," he said, fixing a kind gaze on the two of them, "why don't you tell Officer Banks about the two vases, Mr. Hollis?"

Mr. Hollis looked stunned and whipped his head from side to side. He half rose from his chair, but Michael had already moved over to stand by the door.

Reverend Tom adopted his most calming professional demeanor. "Please, Mr. Hollis. It's okay. We think we have some idea of what has happened, and if we're correct, then I'm confident we can work things out. That's why we're meeting here instead of at the police station."

Anne looked nervously at Michael. He had not been happy about this arrangement and had agreed to it only after a great deal of persuasion by Reverend Tom. For now, though, he merely remained quiet and watchful.

Mr. Hollis had resumed his seat, but he remained quiet, merely licking his lips while his eyes darted about.

Reverend Tom continued, "Tell me, Mr. Hollis, does your uncle know about the two vases?"

Anne looked at Mr. Stratton and was surprised to find that he was staring at his nephew with lively interest and a slight smile.

"No," Mr. Hollis finally said, though it came out as more of a croak. "No, he doesn't."

Reverend Tom nodded. "Perhaps you'd better tell him, then. It might be easier to address him than us. I believe, Mr. Hollis, that you are a dutiful nephew, and you realize you have a responsibility to tell him."

Mr. Hollis turned partly toward his uncle but then quickly dropped his gaze.

"Yeah, Ronnie," Mr. Stratton said. "You heard the parson. Go ahead and tell me." To Anne's ears, his gruff delivery couldn't quite hide a note of amusement in his voice.

Mr. Hollis rested his elbow on the arm of his chair and his forehead against his palm. "Yes, okay. Yes. I'll tell you." He drew a shuddering breath. "I took the vase from the museum. And I replaced it with another one from your collection."

"Did you now?" Mr. Stratton asked softly. Michael stirred but remained silent.

"Thank you, Mr. Hollis," Reverend Tom said softly, "but I think now you also need to explain your reasoning. Why go to all the trouble of replacing the vase, instead of just taking the one that was there?"

Mr. Hollis looked up. "Uncle Percy wanted to help the library," he said, as if this should have been obvious. "I thought they could go ahead and auction the second one instead, and the library would still get the money. And more or less what they'd been expecting."

Apparently Michael could no longer contain himself. "But why go through all that?" he demanded. Why steal one vase and leave behind another of equal value?"

But a direct question from a police officer only had the effect of shutting Mr. Hollis up again.

After a moment, Reverend Tom said, "But it wasn't of equal value, was it?"

Mr. Hollis shook his head.

"Mr. Stratton took the vase to Miles Bridges and told him he thought it was worth about ten thousand dollars," Reverend Tom explained. "Mr. Bridges, a knowledgeable man but not an expert, looked at the vase and concluded that Mr. Stratton's estimate was credible. So that's what the story became—a vase worth ten thousand dollars, donated to benefit the library. But in fact, that particular vase was worth quite a bit more, wasn't it Mr. Hollis? How much more?"

Mr. Hollis groaned and said, "Ten times that. At least." He turned again to his uncle. "Don't you see? I had to get it back. You need that money! Your treatment is only going to get more expensive, not to mention your care, and I just don't have it. You're going to need those resources yourself so that you can be comfortable."

"When I go to that home, you mean," Mr. Stratton said bitterly. "The one you want to send me to."

"It's not about what I want," Mr. Hollis said, frustration edging his voice. "It's about what you need. You shouldn't be living on your own now. Soon, it just won't be possible."

Now it was Mr. Stratton's turn to avert his eyes, and he waved his hand vaguely in a dismissive gesture.

"Look what happened when you fell a few months ago," Mr. Hollis continued.

Mr. Stratton's body stiffened at those words, and he said, "They don't need to hear about that."

"And you know that's not the only thing that's happened," Mr. Hollis added.

Mr. Stratton looked ready to argue further but then sat back, defeated.

Mr. Hollis turned to Reverend Tom. "This way," he said, "I figured Uncle Percy would get to make his donation, even if he didn't realize it came from him. The library would get the money promised to it. And my uncle would still have the most valuable piece of his collection available to convert into cash when he needed it."

"I don't see how you figured that last part," said Michael. "Your uncle wouldn't have the vase, you would."

Mr. Hollis cast a sorrowful look at his uncle, and said, "I just needed to slip it back into his collection when he wasn't looking."

Mr. Stratton fired up again at this. "And you just thought I wouldn't notice, did you?" he demanded angrily. "Think I'm that far gone? How long did you think you'd have to wait before you could 'slip it back in,' as you say? I'll have you know I would have spotted it the instant you returned it! To think I wouldn't know my own vase." He watched as his nephew stared at him for a moment, and then turned away. "What?" he demanded. "What now?"

"But you haven't noticed, Uncle," Mr. Hollis said in a small and pitying voice. "It's already there."

"Hold on," said Michael Banks suddenly. "Bridges and Mr. Stratton here weren't the only two who put that value on the vase. That estimate was verified by an expert."

Reverend Tom nodded. "And that expert was Angie Staub. And you already know that she was attempting to collude with a collector to purchase the vase below its value. You just didn't know how *much* below its value. But I'm sure she did."

"I kept waiting for the news to break about its real value," Mr. Hollis said, "and I couldn't understand why it didn't. If the truth about its value came from someone other than me, there was the chance that Uncle Percy would actually believe it. But even then I wasn't sure what he would do. He might decide that he was honor-bound to stick to the donation rather than ask for it back. But then the news never came out, and I decided I needed to take matters into my own hands."

"And how did you know the vase's value when your uncle did not?" Michael demanded.

"Oh, he knew," Mr. Hollis said reluctantly. "We had a full valuation of the collection done a year or so ago. But Uncle Percy, well, he's kind of stuck on these appraisals he had done years ago, and those are the numbers that have stayed in his mind ever since."

"So there you are, Officer Banks," said Reverend Tom. "You've got one vase that was stolen but which is now back in the possession of its original owner. You've got another vase that was taken without permission but which was intended to fulfill the wishes of the donor in regards to the first vase. And you've got the library, which will probably realize a donation of very much the scale that it had envisioned all along. Anne has told me that the library does not wish to press charges, and I'm going to assume that Mr. Stratton will not do so against his own nephew. It sounds to me like a case of all's well that ends well."

* * *

They tried to convince Mr. Stratton and Mr. Hollis to stay for the auction, but after the revelations of the evening they decided to call it a night. They both thanked Anne for not pressing charges, though in truth, Anne didn't think that she would have had the legal right to do so even if she wanted to.

Reverend Tom walked them back out to their car, leaving Anne and Michael behind in the office.

Michael shook his head. "Well, congratulations, Anne. You figured this all out just because of Stratton's behavior the other day?"

"He was so sure he knew that vase when he saw it in the conference room," Anne said. "He just didn't realize which one it was." After a pause, she continued, "I have to admit, though, I'm still not entirely clear how he managed to do it."

"Oh, he had help," Michael said. "Help from an insider."

Anne looked at him in astonishment. "How do you know that?"

"Well, I had to check into it, didn't I? As soon as you and Reverend Tom came to me on Friday with this crazy theory, I had to try to find some way to corroborate it. Mr. Hollis doesn't live around here, doesn't have access. It stands to reason that he must have had some help. "Turns out he found someone desperate enough for a little extra cash that he was willing to let Mr. Hollis into the museum when no one else was there. With nobody around, it was easy enough to carry in one vase, make the switch, and carry out the other. The only person who might have been in a position to catch him was the person who was helping him."

"One of the extra security guards," Anne exclaimed as the realization dawned. "Was it Theo?"

Michael shook his head. "I'll neither confirm nor deny. The person involved has lost his position, but it looks like he won't have any criminal charges filed, so he can be grateful for that. But I found this person and confirmed your theory. Otherwise, I wouldn't have agreed to this little stunt."

"Well, I know one thing," Anne said with a smile, "the accomplice wasn't Wendy."

"As to that," said Michael, "you have my solemn word that first thing tomorrow, I will call Wendy and officially inform her that, in the matter of the stolen vase, she is not a suspect."

Anne smiled and looked at her watch. "Come on, let's go back to the auction. There should still be a few big-ticket items left, and I don't want to miss seeing Blue Hill's 'auction fever' in action."

About the Author

Emily Thomas is the pen name for a team of writers who have come together to create the series Secrets of the Blue Hill Library. *Sidetracked Suspicions* was written by the wife-and-husband team of Jolyn and William Sharp.

Jolyn is a magazine editor; William is a fund-raiser for a university. After a number of years in New York City, they now live in rural New Hampshire with their cat and dog. Jolyn knits and weaves and likes meeting with other fiber enthusiasts, and William leads book discussions at their local library. They both enjoy mysteries and traveling and finding mysteries that are set in the places they are visiting.

A Conversation with the Authors

Q. *Who is your most interesting relative in your combined Family Tree?*

A. There is a longstanding though unverified rumor in Jolyn's family that they are distantly related to President James Monroe. Who wouldn't want to be related to the man who presided over the Era of Good Feelings?

Q. *Do you have any family heirlooms or antiques in your home? Can you tell us about your favorite?*

A. Alas, we have nothing of great value. We do have some beaded purses that belonged to Jolyn's grandmother and some very fine doilies that she made. And in our attic we have an ancient and non-functioning VCR that will surely be an heirloom someday.

Q. *Aunt Edie's attic appears to hold a limitless inventory of treasure (and junk?). Which of Aunt Edie's attic treasures would you most like to own?*

A. Her books. She'd had such a full life and had met so many interesting people, that we would expect her to have a shelf devoted to first editions personally signed by the authors.

Q. *Do you see yourselves more as packrats, like Aunt Edie, or pitch-it kind of people? Or are you each different in this regard?*

A. We're really only packratish about books, which we find difficult to part with. William even hates to get rid of duplicate copies. (What if you want to loan it to someone?)

Q. *If you were to participate in an* Antiques Roadshow *type of program, what item would you bring for appraisal? Why?*

A. In Jolyn's family are a few paintings that her great grandmother painted that (we think) are quite beautiful. She wasn't a famous artist, but it would be interesting to hear what an art historian would have to say about her craft and style.

Q. *What's the most interesting fact you've learned while researching and writing the Secrets of the Blue Hill Library series?*

A. We were fascinated to learn that the origins of matryoshka dolls are well known. We had thought of them as distinctively Russian folk art and so assumed that their beginnings must be lost in the mists of time. In fact, the first set of dolls was carved in 1890 by Vasily Zvyozdochkin from a design by Sergey Malyutin, who also painted them. The design even won a bronze medal in the Paris Exposition of 1900 (which also saw the introduction of the Ferris Wheel).

Recipes from the Library Guild

Helen Smith's Honey-Oat Banana Bread

A moist, hearty, not-too-sweet bread perfect for coffee hour on a crisp Sunday morning. If you are using nuts, walnuts work as well as pecans. Toast the nuts gently in a toaster oven and let cool before chopping. If you can't find white whole-wheat flour at your grocery store, you can mix a half-cup of unbleached white flour and a half-cup of whole wheat.

1 cup white whole-wheat flour
½ cup rolled oats
¼ cup wheat germ or ground flax seeds
2 teaspoons baking powder
½ teaspoon baking soda
⅓ cup honey
¼ cup applesauce (unsweetened)
½ teaspoon salt
1 cup mashed bananas (about 2½ ripe bananas)
1 large egg
1 teaspoon vanilla extract
½ cup chopped toasted pecans (optional)

Preheat oven to 350 degrees and grease a loaf pan.

Blend together the flour, rolled oats, wheat germ, baking powder, and baking soda in a large bowl and set aside.

Beat together the honey, applesauce, and salt. In a separate bowl, mash the bananas and then stir in the egg and vanilla. Combine with the honey mixture.

Stir the wet ingredients into the dry, stirring just until combined. Fold in nuts, if using. Pour the batter into the loaf pan and bake for fifty to fifty-five minutes, until a toothpick stuck in the center comes out clean. Cool in the pan for five minutes and then turn out onto cooling rack to finish cooling.

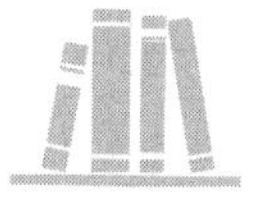

From the Guideposts Archives

This article by Bill Puchstein originally appeared in *Guideposts* magazine.

Our first Sunday morning in Frankfort, Ohio, we dropped in at the Methodist church and my wife, Kay, stood up to announce, "We've just bought the old Sanford house. We'd love to invite everybody to come over next week after church before we start restoring it." Those folks didn't wait a moment. No sooner had the minister said his last Amen the next week than they appeared at our door, welcoming us with casseroles and cut flowers and their memories of what the house looked like under the previous owners. The old-fashioned crank doorbell on our front door rang nonstop.

"You didn't tell me this was Grand Central Station," I remarked to Kay.

"You'll get used to it," she replied.

I wasn't so sure. I'd never lived in a small town before, and Frankfort, Ohio, population one thousand, was the real McCoy. Total strangers called to me on the street, "Hi, Bill!" Women I'd never met before asked about Kay's stoneware collection. She was raised here and her parents were still nearby, but she'd lived away for years. I grew up in suburbia. I figured I was being friendly if I waved to a neighbor watering his lawn or returned a wayward newspaper.

What brought us back to Frankfort was the Sanford place. An 1851 Federal-style farmhouse with a cupola, it was on an old Indian mound smack in the center of town. Kay and I work as antiques dealers, traveling all over the country organizing and promoting shows, so I have a soft spot for beautifully built old things. This house was a real gem. It had fine hand-carved woodwork and handsome high-ceilinged rooms. The Sanford place had even been a stop on the Underground Railroad. When Kay saw that it was for sale, she insisted we look at it. The price was very reasonable.

"With all the travel we do," Kay said, "it'd be nice to come back to a place that has real roots." I had to agree with her. What's more, the house was big enough to store our own antiques and the things we sold in our business. It made good economic sense. Our bid was accepted and we moved in.

That's when I started finding out just how small Frankfort was. Folks would stop me to say how much they liked the color we were painting the living room or how nice they thought our old furniture looked in the place. It was like living in a storefront window. I wondered if they watched to see what we ate for dinner at night. "People are just being neighborly," Kay insisted. "They want you to feel welcome."

I'd feel more welcome, I thought, *if people paid me less mind.* It got so these neighbors didn't even bother cranking that old-fashioned bell. They'd just open the door and holler "Yoo-hoo!" They'd exclaim over Kay's collection of handmade Longaberger baskets or one of our antique Diamond Dyes cabinets.

"Don't you worry," one of them said to Kay. "When you go away we'll keep an eye on the place."

In March 1998, we were in Round Top, Texas, doing one of our biggest antiques shows of the year. As usual, we checked in with Kay's parents. It was a good thing too. There'd been a fire at our house. Neighbors had seen smoke. Three volunteer departments had fought the blaze. *We should drive back tonight,* I thought. We called the fire chief. "Don't come home now," he said. "There's yellow tape all around the place. Until we figure out what caused the fire, we don't want anyone in the house."

That whole week in Texas, Kay and I told everybody who visited our booth the terrible news. I worried about what must have been lost in the fire. Antique quilts, hooked rugs, old oil paintings, the huge country-store cabinets that were a specialty of ours. Not to mention the damage to the place itself. We were lucky it hadn't burnt to the ground. Still I found myself praying over and over, "Dear God, don't let this be the end of us. How would we ever recoup our losses?"

Finally, we got back home to Frankfort. Kay's parents were waiting for us at the house. It was still standing, but the cupola was badly burned. With a sinking feeling, we went inside. The acrid smell of smoke stung my eyes and nose. Everything looked worse than I'd feared. The cherry wood banister we'd restored had been scarred by the fire. The hardwood floors and papered walls were gashed by fire hoses. Old plaster bulged from water damage. Ceiling medallions had crashed to the floor.

I couldn't even say it, but Kay knew what I was thinking. All the things we had collected—all those fine collectibles or just sentimental trinkets—were gone. The nineteenth-century Italian bedroom suite we'd had since the first days of our marriage, an old rocking horse we'd found at a flea market, a child's doll buggy like the one from *Gone With the Wind*. The rooms were empty!

In the stairwell I noticed a waterlogged mattress about three feet thick. "I don't even want to think about the bed," I said. I had a vision of scorched wood.

Kay's father stood next to me. "That mattress is one of the few things the townspeople didn't save," he said.

"What?"

"The whole town showed up. While the fire department was fighting the blaze in the attic and cupola, neighbors carried everything outside. They ripped chandeliers off the ceiling, yanked cupboards off the walls. There was a track meet at the school and the kids rushed over to evacuate your grand piano."

"Where is everything now?" Kay asked.

"After the fire was put out, there was a regular assembly line in your backyard. People cleaned things and put them in boxes. Ladies wiped off water and soot while kids scavenged for storage spots. Everything's still here in town—in garages, trailers, sheds, barns. You'd be amazed. Nothing was chipped or broken."

I thought of the neighbors who were always dropping in. What if they had minded their own business? We'd have no business left! This was how the town of Frankfort, Ohio, population one thousand, practiced the Golden Rule. Neighbors helped neighbors. They'd helped us.

While the house was being restored, we moved into a cabin on the property. We made a big banner and stretched it across the front of the old place. It said in bold blue letters, "Thank You, Frankfort, for Saving Our Home! Bill and Kay." Our neighbors would be the first to see our house when it was fixed up. But they'd know about that as soon as we did. News travels fast around here.

Read on for a sneak peek of another exciting book in Secrets of the Blue Hill Library!

For the Birds

The Blue Hill Library hummed with activity as the members of the Feathered Friends Birders Club filed up the stairs in the beautiful old Victorian. Anne Gibson was just setting out the bowl of pink punch on the refreshment table in the Reference Room when a woman's voice in the hall said in a high-pitched voice, "Spies, I tell you. There are spies right here in Blue Hill."

"Coraline, what on earth are you talking about? What spies?" Another female voice said with a tinge of exasperation.

Anne set the ladle in the bowl and tugged on the plastic film that covered the cookie platter as two women rounded the corner and entered the room. The taller of the two, with graying hair, a hawk-like nose, and black-rimmed glasses was Trudy Conner, chairwoman of the upcoming bird festival. She had requested use of the Reference Room for the Birders Club meeting tonight since their usual place was unavailable.

The shorter woman was Coraline Watson, a neighbor of Anne's friend Mildred. Her green eyes sparkled behind thick glasses, and her cheeks were flushed as she carried a large round bird cage covered with a dark green cloth to the front of the room. Neither woman seemed to notice Anne. Before Anne could say hello, Coraline continued her tirade, "Their spies are right here in Blue Hill," She sat the bird cage on a folding chair. "They are out to stop us."

"Who are *they*?" Trudy took a stack of papers from the colorful canvas bag she carried. "Ray, can you put these out on the chairs?" She handed them to a stocky man dressed in camouflage-print cargo pants and vest coming in the door.

"I suppose so." Ray took the flyers and turned to Coraline. "So who is trying to do what?"

"The Baxter Chemical Company," Coraline said. "They want to snatch the preserve right out from under us. They are trying to sabotage our event in any way they can."

Trudy looked up from digging through her bag again and shook her head. "You can't be serious."

"I'm dead serious. The same blue van keeps passing my house. I saw it again last night. Twice. It slows down as it drives by. If that van passes by my house again tonight, I'm going to copy down the license plate number and report it to the police."

"But why would they bother us?"

"Because if they can sabotage our event, and we don't get pledges, then they know we won't be able to stop them from purchasing the land when our option runs out. You know those flyers that we have been putting up? Someone took a bunch down."

Trudy bit her lower lip. "Well, that can be a problem."

"And look what happened to our usual meeting place."

"A pipe burst," Ray said. "It happens."

"But was it really an accident this time?" Coraline asked with raised eyebrows. "We were lucky to find another meeting place so close to the festival."

Anne wadded up the plastic wrap from the cookie tray and tossed it into a trash can by the door.

Trudy turned and caught sight of her. "Oh hi, Anne. I'm sorry. I didn't see you back there." She walked down the aisle. "The refreshment table looks lovely. I brought some smoked almonds." She reached into her bag again, pulled out a jar and handed it to Anne.

"Have you met Ray Jefferson yet?" Coraline asked Anne. "He's the president of our birder society."

"I don't believe I've had the pleasure. Nice to meet you, Ray," Anne said as she poured the nuts in a small bowl.

"The pleasure is mine," Ray said, offering his hand and giving Anne a firm handshake. "I knew your aunt. I thought it was quite generous that she bequeathed her home to be a library. Thanks for helping us out in a bind."

"You're welcome." Anne smiled. "The bird festival looks like it's going to be lots of fun."

"It should be." He adjusted his round spectacles. "Are you a birder?"

"I don't go out bird watching, but I do have a feeder out in the front yard that I enjoy."

Trudy looked up. "Ray, can you look over the minutes and make sure I didn't leave anything out from our last festival meeting?"

As Trudy and Ray turned away, Anne's five-year-old daughter, Liddie, skipped into the room and stopped short when she saw the refreshment table.

"Can I have a cookie?" Liddie asked Anne.

"Of course you can, if your mother says it's okay," Coraline said before Anne could answer.

Anne gave Liddie a nod. "Take a napkin and be careful not to spill crumbs."

Liddie chose a chocolate chip cookie. "Thank you."

"Do you like birds?" Coraline asked.

Liddie nodded as she took a bite of cookie.

"Well, come look over here. I have a surprise." She crooked a finger at Liddie to motion for her to follow her to the front of the room. Coraline pulled the cover off of the cage, revealing a bright green parrot.

Liddie's eyes widened and she forgot about her cookie. "What a pretty bird."

The parrot gave a squawk and cocked his head as he stared at Liddie with his beady little eyes.

"This is Lorenzo. He's an Amazon Yellow Nap," Coraline said with a beaming smile. "You can come closer, he won't bite you."

Liddie leaned forward so she was face-to-face with the bird. "Does he talk?"

The parrot let out another squawk and Liddie jumped back.

"Oh yes. More than I like at times." Coraline smiled. "He sure fills up my empty house with happy chatter. Tell him hello."

"Hello," Liddie said.

"Hello, hello, hello." Lorenzo cocked his head. "*Whatcha* doing?"

"I was eating a cookie." Liddie giggled. "You're pretty."

The parrot whistled. "Pretty boy."

"Are you a *good* bird, Lorenzo?" Coraline asked.

Lorenzo bobbed up and down, then let out a screech. "Bad bird."

Anne laughed. "I'm sure he can't be that bad. He is so cute."

"Oh, he has his naughty moments," Coraline said with her hands on her hips. "He can also be tricky at times. If I don't lock his cage really securely, he can get the door open. He gets out and there's trouble. He's chewed up one of my favorite lampshades. He had such great fun I almost didn't want to scold him, but now I have to get a new lampshade. I don't really blame him, though."

"How come?" Liddie asked, her gaze firmly on the bird.

"He's been a bit lonely. Poor Lorenzo. He's missing his former owner and his granddaughter, Lacey." She smiled at Liddie. "In fact, you look like her. She has similar brunette curly hair and big brown eyes."

"Why can't his owner have him?" Liddie asked.

"He moved into a retirement center and his roommate is allergic to down." Coraline looked over her shoulder as more people entered the room, filling the chairs. "Liddie, can you do me a favor? Can you keep Lorenzo company later? We're going to have a quick festival committee meeting after the main meeting. Lorenzo makes such noise, and I don't really want to keep him covered up for that long."

Coraline glanced at Anne. "That is, if your mother doesn't mind."

"Of course not," Anne said warmly. We can put him in the Children's Room when you're ready."

Ray had called the meeting to order. Coraline introduced Lorenzo and discussed his unique characteristics, including the fact that yellow-napped parrots are one of the best bird talkers. Besides voices, they could mimic almost anything such as sirens, whistles, and alarms.

"In fact, Lorenzo's previous owner had trained him to be a watch parrot, sort of like a watchdog. He yelled 'danger' when he saw a stranger entering his old home and once scared off a burglar."

"Danger, danger," Lorenzo repeated, and a chuckle went up over the room. "Hello!"

The meeting continued with a slide presentation of some of the local wild birds. "And of course the rare and endangered birds will be harder to find during the bird-watching contest this weekend, which is why they will be worth more points if spotted," Ray said as some of the members took notes.

The general meeting concluded. The club members lingered by the refreshment table, chatting, and then slowly left until about six members remained.

Coraline carried the cage out of the room, and Anne hurried after her. Anne showed Coraline where to place it on a table in the Children's Room. Liddie looked up from her coloring book.

"If Lorenzo gets out, come get me immediately," Coraline said. "He loves books…but not to read," She hurried back across the hall.

"What did she mean, Mommy?" Liddie scooted over closer to the cage.

"I think Lorenzo would like to chew on the books."

"Oh, that would be bad!" Liddie exclaimed. "I'll watch him real good."

"Thanks, sweetie." Anne cast a look at the parrot and noted the clip that held the door shut was in place before stepping across the hall to stand by the door to the Reference Room. From there, she could keep an eye on Liddie and start sorting the cart of books that needed to be shelved.

Inside the Reference Room, Ray said, "Okay, we need to start the committee meeting. Trudy, will you please take over?"

"Yes, we need to have a financial update. Coraline, do you have the treasurer's report?"

"Yes, I have copies right here." She dug into her bag and pulled out several sheets. She shuffled through them once and then again.

Ray cleared his throat. "Is there a problem?"

Coraline looked up. "Oh dear, I left the last page at home with the last of the deposits recorded on it."

Trudy sighed. "Okay, just give us what you have."

"Am I late?" someone whispered behind Anne. She turned to find her old high school friend, Jennifer Banks.

Anne stepped back. "Jennifer, hi! They just started the meeting about the festival. I didn't you know belonged to the birder club."

"I don't, but Trudy is a fellow classroom mother and convinced me to design some of the booths." Jennifer ran her fingers through her spiky red hair. "I took a nap after supper and overslept. Ever since Jed got a paper route, I've been getting up at the crack of dawn with him."

"How's he doing with it?" Anne asked. Jed, thirteen, was the oldest of Jennifer's three children.

"He's doing great considering this is all new to him. I just can't seem to sleep when one of my babies is out and about." She yawned. "I better get in there before I'm really missed."

"Coraline, you have the trophies, correct?" Trudy asked.

"They are not in yet. They had to special-order the bird medallions that go on them."

Ray pushed his glasses higher on his nose as he turned to Coraline. "This is not good. Those trophies should've been ordered a lot sooner, and we should have used a local shop. We only have four days left!"

"Stop worrying. I got a great deal by going with this other store. I'll just drive over to Appleton and get them myself when they're finished," Coraline said with a huff in her voice.

Ray frowned. "You better, or this will be a disaster. I knew I should've…"

"Jennifer, how are the booths coming?" Trudy asked, deftly cutting off Ray's complaint.

"Well, I brought some final sketches for you to see. Tomorrow I'll pick up the fabric if you approve of the design." She pulled a sketchbook out of her bag. I jotted down the cost of the fabric and decorations. I was able to get Bethany's Fabrics to donate some of their remnants, so that will help."

Anne carried books into the Children's Room. Liddie had a book on her lap and she was reading to Lorenzo. The parrot sat on its perch close to Liddie, his head cocked as if listening intently.

Anne had finished shelving the books for the second floor and was straightening up when the meeting concluded. Jennifer popped out first and waved at Anne. "Gotta run. See you at the festival."

"Bye!" Anne waved at her friend as Jennifer dashed down the hall. She helped Trudy and Coraline clean up the refreshment table, and then they trooped downstairs.

"Bye, Lorenzo. I'll miss you," Liddie said.

"You can come over to visit him anytime you'd like." Coraline set the parrot cage by the door as she hunted in her purse. "Now, what did I do with my keys? Ah, here they are." She smiled at Anne. "Your aunt would have surely enjoyed the festival. She really loved those birds she had. In fact..."

A screech sounded and a flurry of green feathers swooped by Anne's head. She ducked. Lorenzo had gotten out of the cage. He circled the room twice and landed on the checkout counter by Liddie.

"Hello. Hello." Lorenzo bowed his head.

"You naughty bird!" Coraline rushed over. The bird nimbly avoided Coraline's outstretched hand and moved closer to Liddie. He bowed his head again, his feathers ruffling. Liddie looked questioningly at Coraline.

"I'm sorry," Coraline said. "Looks like I need to get his wings clipped again. Usually I just get one wing clipped so he spirals to the ground, but obviously he can fly well enough now."

Lorenzo bowed his head again. "What is he doing?" Liddie asked.

"He wants to be stroked on top of his head. Lacey used to do that every evening when she was visiting her grandfather. He doesn't deserve to be petted after escaping, but go ahead if you want to," Coraline said with a huff.

Liddie reached out with her index finger and touched the bird lightly on the head. He moved closer to Liddie.

"See? He really must like you," Coraline said as a ringing came from her purse. "Excuse me." She pulled out the phone and put it to her ear and listened. "You're kidding? That's so exciting. Can I call you right back?"

Coraline held her arm out to Lorenzo and, with some reluctance, he hopped on it. She stuffed him back in his cage, clipped the door shut, and firmly pulled on the cover.

"Bye-bye," a soft voice said as Coraline headed to the door.

"Bye, Lorenzo," Liddie called. "I hope I can see you again."

"Thanks, Anne, for helping tonight. Sorry to run." She rushed out the door. "Bye, everyone."

Lorenzo squawked. "Bad bird."

Liddie giggled and picked a long green feather off the floor and smoothed it with her fingers. "I want a parrot."

"He was fun, wasn't he? Now it's time to wash up and get ready for bed. If you hurry, you and Ben can watch a video," Anne said in an effort to distract her animal-loving daughter from begging for a bird. "I'll make some popcorn. Does that sound good?"

"Can I pick the movie?"

"We'll see. Ben might already be watching something." Anne couldn't remember who had chosen a video the last time, and she hoped the kids wouldn't argue about it.

"Okay." Liddie headed back up the stairs to the second floor, which led to the entrance of their private residence. The kids didn't have school the rest of the week due to a teacher's conference, so Anne could allow them to stay up a bit later than usual.

Anne closed up the library and turned out lights as she checked each of the four rooms on the first floor and then trudged up the stairs to the second. She stopped by the Reference Room and noticed some tiny downy feathers drifting across the floor. The parrot must be molting. She again wondered what Coraline had meant about Aunt Edie and her love of birds. Anne had spent most of her childhood traipsing in and out of the old mansion. Her family had only lived four blocks away. Sometimes she even spent the night here when her mother's job as a nurse and her father's accounting career often kept them working late.

Although Anne had made some interesting discoveries about Aunt Edie's activities since moving back to Blue Hill, there was a possibility that Coraline was mistaken about her aunt keeping birds. And she certainly hoped Coraline was mistaken about the chemical company spying and trying to sabotage the festival. The other members of the festival community acted like they weren't worried.

Anne picked up the punch bowl and ladle. She'd wash them tonight and return them to the storage closet in the morning. She let herself through the doorway at the end of the hall, which opened to their private living room and kitchen, and put the punch bowl in the sink. As the sink filled with soapy water, she got out the popcorn and popped it in the microwave. Feet pounded on the floor overhead.

The rest of the evening sped by. Anne caught up on some library paperwork while Ben and Liddie enjoyed their movie and popcorn. By the time the movie ended, Anne's eyes drooped. It had been a long day. She shooed the children upstairs to brush their teeth.

Anne straightened up the living room and kitchen and made sure the doors were locked before heading up to the second floor. Liddie was already in bed. She had pulled out a children's pop-up book about Creation, and it lay open on her lap to the page that featured brightly colored birds. She looked up at Anne. "I'm glad God didn't skip the fifth day of creation. That's when He made the birds."

"I'm glad too." Anne sat on the chair beside the bed. "Is that the book you want me to read today?"

Liddie nodded and scooted farther down into bed.

Anne took the book and paged to the front. "In the beginning..." She read through to the end, and Liddie's eyelids were drooping. They had their nightly prayers together, and Anne tucked Liddie in. She kissed her daughter on the forehead and closed the door until it was almost shut. She loved this nightly routine with Liddie. Ben joined them sometimes, but he was starting to be more independent, reading to himself at bedtime. She popped into his bedroom. Ben's chocolate Lab, Hershey, was already curled up at the end of Ben's bed, sleeping. Anne had a quick time of prayer with Ben before she retired to her own room.

Anne quickly went through her evening routine and crawled under the quilt. She felt as though she had been asleep for only a few minutes when Liddie yelled. "Mom, come quick!"

Anne hopped up, momentarily confused. Dawn was breaking beyond the window and cast a gray light in the bedroom. She raced into the hall and to Liddie's bedroom.

Liddie stood in the middle of her dark room and pointed at the window. "Mommy! Look, it's Lorenzo."

The green and yellow bird clung to the outside of the screen, his head bobbing back and forth. He let out a screech and flapped his wings. "Cora. Coraline. Danger. Danger!"

A Note from the Editors

We hope you enjoy Secrets of the Blue Hill Library, created by the Books and Inspirational Media Division of Guideposts, a nonprofit organization that touches millions of lives every day through products and services that inspire, encourage, help you grow in your faith, and celebrate God's love in every aspect of your daily life.

Thank you for making a difference with your purchase of this book, which helps fund our many outreach programs to military personnel, prisons, hospitals, nursing homes, and educational institutions. To learn more, visit GuidepostsFoundation.org.

We also maintain many useful and uplifting online resources. Visit Guideposts.org to read true stories of hope and inspiration, access OurPrayer network, sign up for free newsletters, download free e-books, join our Facebook community, and follow our stimulating blogs.

To learn about other Guideposts publications, including the best-selling devotional *Daily Guideposts*, go to ShopGuideposts .org, call (800) 932-2145, or write to Guideposts, PO Box 5815, Harlan, Iowa 51593.